Princes & Kings

A ROSE IN A THORN BUSH

BOOK ONE

SYDNEY WILLIAMS

Princes & Kings

tellwell

Tellwell Talent
www.tellwell.ca

ISBN
978-0-2288-6346-5 (Hardcover)
978-0-2288-6345-8 (Paperback)
978-0-2288-6347-2 (eBook)

Characters

Llywelyn the Great; Loo-elyn: Ruler of Gwynedd, Wales.

Dafydd ap Llywelyn; Dav-ith ap Loo-elyn: Eldest son of Llywelyn the Great.

Gruffudd ap Llywelyn; Grif-ith ap Loo-elyn: Second son of Llywelyn the Great.

Sanena; Sa-ne-na; Wife to Gruffudd ap Llywelyn and daughter of Caradog ap Tomas.

Caradog ap Tomas; Car-a-dog: Lord of Anglecey, Wales and father of Sanena.

Owain ap Gruffudd; O-wine ap Grif-ith: Eldest son of Gruffudd ap Llywelyn and Sanena.

Llywelyn ap Gruffudd; Loo-elyn ap Grif-ith: Second eldest son of Gruffudd ap Llywelyn and Sanena.

Dafydd ap Gruffudd; Dav-ith ap Grif-ith: Third son of Gruffudd ap Llywelyn and Sanena.

Rhodri ap Gruffudd; Ro-dree ap Grif-ith: Fourth and youngest son of Gruffudd ap Llywelyn and Sanena.

PLACE NAMES

Gwynedd: Goo-yn-eth.
Clwyd: Cloo-id.
Aberfraw: Aber-vra-oo.
Snodonia: Snow-don-eea.

Dedication

This book is dedicated to my grade 12 history teacher, John Ringstead, who first introduced me to the character of Llywelyn and to my Business Abilities Coach, Louise Doyle for encouraging me to write this story, and to Wendy Tarasoff for her help with the editing of this book. I would also like to thank my family who has always supported me in everything I do.

I don't think I would have had the courage to write this story without all of you.

So thank you.

Chapter 1

A Funeral to Remember

The town of Aberfraw Castle in the Valley of Clwyd Snowdonia, Gwynedd, Wales in the year 1240 AD

It was a cold, damp afternoon. In the town of Aberfraw Castle, all of Gwynedd wails as a procession of finely dressed nobles carried the coffin of the late King of Gwynedd, Llywelyn, the Great, through the streets. From all over the land, Gwynedd's subjects arrived: they came to look upon the face of their dead King and to mourn his passing. The cobbles, slippery from a powerful rainstorm the night before, hampered the procession of nobles as they prepared to lay him to rest. The sky was still overcast with clouds that promised more rain as if nature was mourning for the great man. Filthy street urchins roughly shoved through the crowds of people, trying to catch a glimpse of the nobles while more fortunate children sat upon the shoulders of their father to see the royal party in their fine outfits.

Leading the royal procession were the King's two sons, Dafydd ap Llywelyn and Gruffudd ap Llywelyn.

Gruffudd, the King's younger and illegitimate son, had no claim to the throne. He didn't mind; he had never wanted to be a ruler. Gruffudd preferred being the head warrior of the royal army, protecting the people of the land in that way. It gave him a sense of freedom somehow that he felt being ruler would not. He was resplendently dressed as any noble should be in a thick green wool tunic, wool leggings tucked at the knee with high leather boots. His height and physique gave him an air of command and respect, both on the battlefield and off it, and gained him a lot of respect with the people of the land.

Gruffudd's wise gray eyes turned towards his wife, Senana, who walked beside him with her head held high, giving her an air of great confidence. She felt him looking at her and caught his eye with a loving smile. Smiling back, he felt blessed to have such a woman by his side. From the moment they first met, he had known that she was the woman he would marry. Her light brown hair fell in the way that he liked, in a single braid that snaked down the back of her dress. Her dark-green silk skirt complimented his tunic and set off her deep blue eyes nicely. Such eyes any man in love could easily get lost in.

The heavy air wasn't helping his somber mood. Instead, Gruffudd felt like it weighed heavily down on his heart, finding it hard to breathe. He had loved his father very much and would miss him terribly. He felt the loss of his father like a dagger to the heart. But he would not cry. He told himself that he had to stay strong for his children who must also be feeling the loss of their grandfather. He felt blessed that he had at least been able to say goodbye to him.

"I am so sorry my love," she said, placing her hand on his arm in sympathy. "Are you all right?"

He gave her a weak smile in return and placed his large hand on her so much smaller one. "I will be all right in time. It is just a shock," Gruffudd said.

"I know. It is hard to believe your father is gone," she soothed.

"He was a great man; he will be sorely missed." She nodded her head in agreement.

"We will all miss his smiling face. He was quite the joker in his day," she said with a smile.

"He was that," he agreed. "He was also one of the greatest warriors the land has ever seen and he loved you very much."

"I know," she said. "So did your mother. I will miss them both very much. At least they are together again at long last."

"Yes, they are, and I am happy for them. But I will still miss them," he said taking her hand off his arm and placing it in his own as they continued walking along behind the coffin.

As the royal party moved through the streets, one of the young street urchins darted up to Lord Owain, the eldest son of Lord Gruffudd, and attempted to slip his hand into his pocket. Owain quickly grabbed the boy and shook him roughly. "Have some respect," he snapped.

Hearing the altercation, Gruffudd turned his head and smiled at the boy. He reached into his pocket and pulled out a coin, tossing it to the boy.

"Run along now and remember to have more respect for your superiors in the future," he said, giving him a cuff to the arm. The boy, red-faced nodded his head in thanks and ran back into the crowd.

"Why did you do that?" Owain asked.

"Because now he will go on his way and not bother us again," Gruffudd explained.

Owain simply shook his head in disgust, and with a surly look towards the crowd, rubbed his hands on his tunic. The boy's clothing had been so filthy that he could feel the dirt coating his fingers.

His brother, Llywelyn, Gruffudd's second eldest son turned to his brother Owain and cuffed him on the shoulder. "Lighten up," he said with a smile.

Owain gave him a dirty look. "Will you ever grow up and act your age?" he asked grumpily.

"I think I am doing just fine. Why don't you grow up?" Llywelyn said, giving his brother a playful shove. Owain shrugged and shoved him back, causing Gruffudd to turn his head and look at his two sons.

"That is enough from the two of you! This funeral procession is not a party," he scolded and turned his head around to the front once more. Sanena squeezed her husband's fingers lightly and smiled at him with a twinkle of amusement in her eyes.

"They are just getting out their nerves," she said calmly. "Remember they were both very close to their grandfather."

"I know that," Gruffudd said. "But that doesn't mean they are allowed to act like a couple of children."

"You need to relax," she said, giving his fingers another light squeeze. "Everyone is a little tense right now. I am sure, after the funeral, we will all feel much better."

"I am sure you are right," he said, giving her a small smile.

She answered his smile with one of her own, trying to express all of her feelings for him with her smile.

As he walked along, he began to think about his two eldest sons. They were so alike in so many ways. Both were of a similar height and had the same dark gray eyes and the same medium-length dark red hair. They even had the same swing to their step when they walked. They were both experts in the long and short sword as well as the bow, giving them their muscular arms, upper bodies, and strong muscular legs.

Llywelyn had a scar on his cheek from when Owain had cut him in a sword practice session when he was about 13. Llywelyn, with his tendency to be loud and raucous, would get himself into trouble more often than not. It had driven him and Sanena mad, so they had sent him off for warrior training in the royal army. It had served to cool his passions just enough to make him one of the best warriors in his grandfather's army, and the best tracker in the land at only 17. He was incredibly proud of the lad and how far he had come in only a few short years. He had a good head on his shoulders that Gruffudd was sure would help him do great things.

Llywelyn looked behind him to see if his two younger brothers, Dafydd, and Rhodri were keeping up with the procession. Rhodri, the youngest at only six, shuffled along with his head bent to avoid seeing the number of people surrounding the royal party. He was very shy and didn't like big crowds; he wanted nothing more than to be at home playing swords with Dafydd.

Dafydd poked him in the side in frustration at his slowness.

"Ow!" Rhodri pouted.

"Could you possibly walk a little faster, so we get to the square before next Christmas?" Dafydd snapped at his younger brother.

"Leave me alone," Rhodri sniffed.

Catching the conversation, Llywelyn turned his head to look at his younger brothers. "What is going on?" he asked.

"Rhodri is walking too slowly," Dafydd complained.

"I am not," Rhodri protested.

"I know you don't like big crowds," Llywelyn soothed. "But today is a big day. You loved grandfather, right?"

"Yes," Rhodri mumbled.

"I know that he loved you too, and he would want you to be here to say goodbye to him today. So buck up all right?" he admonished.

"Okay," Rhodri agreed.

"That a boy," Llywelyn said, smiling at him. Rhodri made a face that made Dafydd crack a grin of his own. Laughing at his little brother's antics, Llywelyn turned his head back around and faced the front once more.

"What was that all about?" Owain asked.

"Rhodri is afraid of the crowds," Llywelyn explained.

"He has always been shy," Owain agreed.

"I know," Llywelyn said. "Oh, look we are here."

The procession entered the town center, followed by the crowds, and stopped in the middle of the square. The coffin was placed on a raised platform. The people crowded around the platform, talking amongst themselves.

Llywelyn looked up at the clouds in the sky and wondered how long the rain would hold off. He hoped it would leave off at least until the service was over, so they didn't all get soaked while they tried to lay the King to rest. His brother Owain stood, staring at the coffin with tears in his eyes. Llywelyn saw the look of desolation on his brother's face; he wanted to put his arm around his shoulders in sympathy; but, they were both too old for that now. So he stood beside his brother and stared at the coffin.

"I can't believe he is gone," Owain said in a voice cracked with emotion.

"I know," Llywelyn soothed. "Grandfather was so sick in the end that death was more of a blessing than a curse."

"That is true enough," said Owain, wiping his eyes on his sleeve.

"There will never be anyone else like him though," Llywelyn said. "He was one of a kind."

"Oh, I don't know," Owain said. "I think our father is just as good as grandfather ever was."

"He is still not grandfather," Llywelyn argued.

"I suppose you are right," Owain grudgingly agreed.

Rhodri felt a slight chill, hugging his arms around himself; he looked up for just a moment and saw the crowds of people filling the square. Scared, he stepped behind his brother Dafydd and tried to make himself invisible.

Dafydd turned his head and smiled at him; reaching back he gave his shoulder a light squeeze. "It's all right. No one will hurt you," Dafydd assured him.

Rhodri shook his head and hugged himself more tightly.

"I want mother," he whined.

"Mother is at the front with father," Dafydd said. "We can't go to her now."

"Then I want to go home," Rhodri insisted.

"We can't do that either," Dafydd said sympathetically.

"But I don't want to be here. There are too many people," Rhodri complained.

Dafydd gave his brother's shoulder another light squeeze. "I know, but I am sure this won't take too long, and then we can go home again. You just need to hold on a little longer. Can you do that for me?"

"I guess," Rhodri grudgingly agreed.

"That a boy. Oh, get a look at our uncle. Doesn't he look fine in his outfit?" Dafydd said, pointing at Dafydd, the elder, who had just stepped up beside the coffin.

"Yes, he does," Rhodri agreed. Dafydd was not a very tall man, a little over five feet with short-cropped dark red hair, and gray eyes the exact shade of his brother's. He had a thin whip-like body much like his younger namesake and a thin triangular face. He looked out at the crowd; he smiled to see all the people gathered there to pay their respects to their late King. He was touched to see just how loved his father had been, and how much of an influence he had been as ruler; he hoped for his own sake that he would grow to be just as loved by the people as his father had been.

He cleared his throat and raised his hands for silence. Slowly, as people began to notice him, the crowd began to settle down and grow quiet. Owain noticed his uncle standing there beside the coffin with his hands raised and gave a snort. "Gather round people. The slime will speak," he said under his breath.

"What was that?" Llywelyn asked, shooting his brother a suspicious look.

"Nothing," Owain lied.

"Sure," Llywelyn scoffed. He shook his head and waited to hear what his uncle had to say. He knew full well that Owain and their uncle did not get along. In all honesty, he didn't blame Owain for his dislike of the man. Their uncle was not battle worn like their father, and he had always looked down on their mother, Sanena. He hoped that Owain wouldn't do anything stupid. He did tend to be hot-headed and speak out when it would be better to keep quiet.

Dafydd took a deep breath in and then let it out again. He had never been one for big speeches, but he knew how important it was to assure the people that even though their King was gone, they were not alone. He took one last deep breath, and then with a reassuring smile on his face that he didn't truly feel, he began to speak.

"My people," he began, surprised at the steadiness of his voice despite the turmoil inside, "Today is a sad day. For here lies the body of our late King, and my father." All eyes were turned to him now as he stood there beside the coffin with his fine brown silk clothing looking almost black in the dim afternoon sunlight. He blinked his eyes rapidly three times to keep from showing the tears that were just waiting to fall the moment he lost control. But he was ruler now, and he must keep his head for the sake of his people. So he cleared his throat and continued.

"You don't need to have any fears though for I will not let you down."

Llywelyn shook himself like a horse shaking off a fly. "What on earth is that supposed to mean?" he asked no one in particular.

"I don't know," Owain replied. "Nothing good I'd wager."

"In three days," Dafydd continued, "I will take the crown and become your leader. I vow to be as good a ruler as I can possibly be. Have faith in me, and I will not let you down." The crowd erupted in cheers. Their worries assuaged they could sleep soundly in their beds again knowing that their land was once more safe from the English invaders.

Llywelyn watched Owain's face growing red with suppressed anger. He himself didn't know what to make of his uncle's declaration. Would he be a good leader for the people of Gwynedd? It was too soon to tell. He hoped that he would be, not only for his own sake, but also for all these people that would be looking to him for guidance and support now. He was glad it wasn't him.

Seeing the look on his brother's face, Llywelyn reached out and placed his hand on his shoulder, bringing his brother's attention on to him instead. He smiled at him, but Owain didn't return the smile. "Are you all right?" he asked, giving his shoulder a squeeze.

"Who does he think he is kidding? He can't possibly rule. It should be father and not that fraud leading us," Owain said, throwing up his hands in frustration.

"I know," Llywelyn soothed. "But father is not the true heir."

"So what?" Owain exclaimed. "That doesn't change the fact that father would be the better ruler here."

"You are right," Llywelyn agreed. "But it is the way it is, and we can't change that fact."

Owain shook his head. "We will just have to see about that," he said.

Llywelyn had a sudden bad feeling. He looked his brother straight in the face and demanded, "Owain, what are you up to?"

"I am going to tell the people the truth," Owain said, staring right back at his brother in defiance.

"Owain, don't," Llywelyn pleaded, moving his hand from his shoulder to his arm to try and keep him from leaving and causing a scene with their uncle.

"Take your hand off me," Owain demanded.

Llywelyn let go of his arm and stood back, giving him one of his best, "Don't even think about it," looks.

Owain glared at him and shook his head.

"Owain, please don't do this," Llywelyn implored.

"I have to," Owain insisted.

"No, you don't," Llywelyn argued. "Think about what grandfather would have wanted."

"Well, one thing I know is that he wouldn't have wanted is for that fraud to be our next ruler," Owain said, turning away from his brother, he began moving through the crowd.

With a great sense of unease, Llywelyn followed at a safe distance if fists started flying. At this point, he didn't know what his brother would do. As they pushed their way through the crowd, Llywelyn felt the first drops of rainfall, and looking upwards he saw the clouds ready to open up and start pouring down on them all. All thoughts of the weather were wiped from his mind when he saw his brother walking straight up to their uncle where he stood beside the coffin with their mother and father standing beside him.

"Who do you think you are?" Llywelyn heard his brother demand as he rushed up to the little group beside the coffin.

"What are you on about?" Dafydd asked in exasperation.

"Tell these people the truth. Or are you not man enough to do so?" Owain said with a glare.

Dafydd glared back at him in turn," I am the son of our late King, and in three days I will become your new ruler, so you better learn to watch your tone young man," he said.

"Why can't you admit that you are not fit to rule here? How can you let these poor people think for one minute that you could be anything like grandfather was?"

"For your information, I don't plan to do anything of the sort," Dafydd said. "I plan to make my own mark as ruler of Gwynedd."

"I will accept you as ruler over my dead body," Owain snarled.

Having reached the little group at last, Llywelyn inserted himself between his brother and his uncle, effectively stopping his brother from attacking their uncle with anything more than his words. He gave his brother his best, "Shut up before you do any more damage" look and turned his attention to Dafydd.

"Take no notice of him, uncle. He is just upset that his grandfather has died. You can understand, can't you?"

Owain glared at his brother's back.

"Quite right," Gruffudd agreed. "Everyone's nerves get a little frayed during such things. Llywelyn, why don't you take your brother back to the castle to get some rest? It has been a hard afternoon for all of us."

"Yes, of course, father. Come on," Llywelyn said, taking Owain by the arm to lead him back through the crowded square.

"You are a lucky young man that I am not ruler yet," Dafydd said, causing Owain to turn back to him once more. "But you better watch what you say to me from now on. I won't be so forgiving next time." Owain gave his uncle a scathing look, and before he could reply, Llywelyn took a firmer grip on his arm and marched him away.

Dafydd watched him go with a feeling of relief. The problem with Owain's words was that they were the same words he had been saying to himself ever since his father had fallen ill and it had become clear he would not recover. It was deeply unsettling to hear them out loud like that though.

"He has spirit that one," he remarked to Gruffudd.

"Yes, he does," Gruffudd agreed.

"Llywelyn, on the other hand, he is a born diplomat isn't he?"

"Yes," Gruffudd said with a small smile.

"It is all very interesting," Dafydd made a mental note to keep an eye on the two young men: It was clear to him that if he played things right they could both become very useful to him in the future. He had never really been one for the battlefield, but he did have a good head for matters of state, and he knew how to use people. He had watched his father doing such things over the years and had learned what he could. He told himself that he had been training for this day since he was small and that he was ready. He may not have fought as many battles as his brother, but he had fought enough to know how military tactics worked. So why did he feel like he had a colony of snakes writhing in his stomach now? He hadn't had long enough to prepare for this moment. He, why hadn't he ask more questions when his father was alive? What was he thinking? He shook himself mentally and turned to his brother.

"We should put him in the ground before these clouds open up," he said.

"Yes, I think you are right," Gruffudd agreed.

They picked the coffin from the platform and started towards the burial ground that lay a short distance from the town square between the town and the village beyond.

Chapter 2

Sanctuary in Flight

The clouds opened up and the rain that the clouds had been promising all afternoon began to pour down on the two brothers as they walked along the road that led away from the town square back towards Aberfraw Castle. Llywelyn turned his head as they walked and gave his brother a look.

"What were you thinking antagonizing him like that?" he asked.

"He needed to hear the truth," Owain countered angrily.

"No, he didn't," Llywelyn said. Owain said nothing and simply glared at his brother. "When will you learn to keep your big mouth shut?"

"Shut up," Owain growled.

"I see you are not denying it," Llywelyn observed. Owain stopped walking and Llywelyn stopped as well.

"Do you want a fight?" Owain demanded angrily. "Because I will take you right here and now."

Llywelyn shook his head. "No, I don't. That wouldn't solve anything," Llywelyn said calmly. "Come on... let's get back to the castle before we get completely soaked." Llywelyn gave his brother a smile and started walking once more.

"Why is it that you are always so obstinately reasonable?" Owain said falling in to step beside his brother.

"I am not," Llywelyn protested.

"Yes you are," Owain said.

Llywelyn shrugged. "Why is it then that our parents sent me away for training at 13 years old if I wasn't causing any problems?" he insisted.

"You were 13," Owain said. "Everyone is difficult at that age. I was the same, and I am sure father was just as bad when he was that age as well."

"There's a thought," Llywelyn said with a small smile.

"My point is that you were much calmer as when you were a child. Much more like you are now. Whereas I have always tried my best to the biggest pain in the backside could be."

Llywelyn burst out laughing at these words.

Owain tried for a second to keep a straight face, but then gave it up and started laughing as well. They finished the walk up the road to the castle laughing harder than they had in months and getting soaked from the rain that was pouring down from the clouds in the sky.

They reached the castle gates a short time later and Llywelyn returned the guards' respectful nods with one of his own. The gates were opened for the two brothers, and they walked through into the castle courtyard beyond.

The gates shut behind them as they walked together up to the front doors of the castle, where they were met by yet another guard. The man was a little over five feet tall, of pure muscle, with short-cropped gray hair and light green eyes. He gave the brothers a courteous bow of the head as he held the door open for them.

"Good afternoon, my Lords. Did the funeral go well then?"

"As well as could be expected, thank you, Cammo," Llywelyn said with a nod of his own to the guard that had been opening the door for him since he was a small child. He had been a soldier for a time in the royal army for a time but after being injured in a battle, he had returned to guard the castle instead.

"That is good to hear. Your grandfather was a great man, and we will all miss him," Cammo said.

"Yes, we will," Owain agreed.

Cammo pulled the door open all the way and the two brothers walked through into the front hall. Owain headed directly for his room.

Llywelyn watched him go with a smile on his face. They would be all right in the end. As long as they could laugh everything would be all right. As he turned to start down the hall towards his room, he caught the eye of a young kitchen maid peaking around the corner. He had seen her once before watching him with her long black hair and azure eyes that seemed to stare right into him, which made him feel a little funny. He smiled at her and winked; she blushed and ducked back around the corner once more. He shrugged and shook his head in confusion. He would never understand girls.

Feeling the need for a hot bath, and a good meal, he started walking down the hallway towards his room. It had been a hard day, but he didn't plan to stay at home for long. In the morning, he decided he would head into the Welsh countryside to get away and clear his head. Whenever he was troubled, he would take his horse, Arling, and ride off, he didn't care where, sometimes for weeks at a time until he felt clear enough in both body and mind to return home once more. He had always found the fresh air a balm to his nerves when he was upset over something that had been said or done that he had no control over. He had learned a long time ago that when he was feeling like blowing up it was better just to leave and go away for a while until he felt like himself again. Owain talked about him being reasonable and diplomatic, but in reality he was just as angry and confused as his brother most of the time. He just chose to take himself away and work through his feelings rather than let them burst out of him in anger at random.

He smiled at the thought of his horse. Arling was his pride and joy. He had raised her from a small filly and had trained her himself. Now she was one of the best war-horses in the land, never shying away from danger, and Llywelyn trusted her to carry him through any battle. She was always a brave companion wherever he went, and he always grateful to have her by his side.

Reaching his bedroom door, Llywelyn opened it and went inside. Sitting by the fire was his man-servant Olan, busy cleaning one of his many surcoats. A smallish man, Olan made up for his lack of height with a muscular body. His short black hair, and deep-set lake blue eyes, seemed to see everything, giving him an-other-worldly appearance. This ability to see through any situation had come in handy more than once over the years. He looked up when the door opened and saw Llywelyn standing there dripping wet from the rain. Upon seeing him, Olan put down the surcoat and stood up, giving him a small bow. Llywelyn smiled at him."Very funny Olan," he said. Olan smiled back.

"The storm got you then?" he said.

"Yes," Llywelyn said, peeling off his very wet coat, the one he wore for special occasions, and handing it to Olan. "The skies opened up as Owain and I were walking back to the castle."

"I was wondering why you have come back so early," Olan said hanging the coat on a hook by the fire to dry.

"Father sent us back early," Llywelyn explained.

"Why don't you sit down, and I will pour you a cup of brandy," Olan suggested.

"That would be great. Thank you, Olan," and Llywelyn sat down by the fire.

Olan walked to a small table that sat in the corner of the room and picked up the decanter that sat upon it and poured brandy into two cups. He carried these back to the fire and handed one to Llywelyn before sitting down and taking a sip of his own.

"What happened then?" he asked. Llywelyn took a long swallow of brandy before speaking. He placed the cup on the ground beside his chair and pulled off his wet boots in relief. Then, he picked up his cup once more and turned to face his man-servant and overall friend and companion.

"My uncle happened," he said taking another sip of brandy. "Dafydd has declared himself the new ruler of Gwynedd, and he will take the crown in three days time."

"Did they put your grandfather to rest then?"

"I assume so. We left before they buried him," Llywelyn said with a shrug.

"How did the people take your uncle's news then?"

"The people loved it. Owain caused a bit of a scene though. That is why we are back early."

"What did he do?" Olan asked intrigued.

"He walked right up to our uncle and told him he wasn't fit to rule," Llywelyn said with a small smile.

Olan laughed. "That sounds like something he would do," Olan said still laughing.

Llywelyn grinned. "I managed to fix the situation though before it got too out far out of hand though, and father thought it best if I got Owain out of there before he had a chance to do anything more and land himself in a lot of trouble."

"What about you?" Olan asked.

"What about me?"

"Do you think he can do it?"

"I don't know. Maybe," Llywelyn said taking another sip of his brandy.

"What do you want to do? I am assuming you don't want to be here when your uncle takes the crown, Olan observed.

"No, I don't," Llywelyn agreed. "You up for a ride in the country?"

"Sure, Joh could use the exercise." Joh was the horse that Olan rode most often. The two horses got on well, so it made riding together easy.

"Great," Llywelyn said. "We will leave in the morning. Right now though I would kill for a bath and a hot meal."

"That can be arranged," Olan said, picking up the large kettle he used for washing the floor and leaving the room to fill it with water.

Llywelyn drained his cup, and walking over to the table, placed his now empty cup on it. He put some more wood on the fire.

Olan returned a few moments later carrying the now full kettle and walking over to the fire set it to boil. Then he turned and left the room once more in search of food.

Llywelyn opened the small trunk that sat at the end of his bed and pulled out a washcloth and some soap. He laid them on the bedside table. Once the water in the kettle had boiled, he poured it into a large water basin that he had pulled into the middle of the room, and then stripping off his wet clothes, he slid into the steaming hot bath and began to wash. Reveling in the heat of the water as it ran down his body, warming him through for the first time all day. When he was finished, he dried himself off and pulled on fresh clothing. There was no better feeling than to be clean and dry.

As Olan walked through the hallways to the kitchen in search of supper for himself and Llywelyn, as well as enough foodstuffs to last at least three weeks on the road, he began to think about the years he had spent here with his lord. Lord Gruffudd had found him living in an orphanage when he was 11 years old and had brought him back to the castle to be Llywelyn's companion. His parents had died when he was quite young, and he had stayed there until that wonderful day when Lord Gruffudd decided to visit the orphanage. Olan owed everything to Lord Gruffudd. He had saved his life that day. Olan hadn't grown very much as a child, and so the other bigger children had picked on him a lot. Since he had come to the castle, he hadn't been picked on by anyone, not even once, and now here he was five years later the companion of one of the best warriors in all of Gwynedd and he was being treated with respect instead of scorn.

As he entered the kitchen, he was greeted by a wall of heat and the mouth-watering smell of roasting meat. All five of the kitchen's fires were going. Some of the fires had large kettles hanging over them with some kind of delicious substance in them that bubbled enticingly, while others had everything from beef to pork and even what looked like mutton roasting on spits. The smells in the kitchen were making his mouth water, and his stomach gave a large gurgle. It had been a while since he had last eaten anything.

Elsa, the head cook, was hard to miss with her muslin apron and her blond hair done up in a tight bun at the back of her head, giving her face a bit of an austere look about it with her close-set brown eyes that could cut down even the bravest of kitchen boys with a single stare. She was a fairly short woman with strong muscular arms that she got from handling all these heavy pots and hunks of meat. She could pick up half a cow all on her own if she wanted to, and Olan had even seen her do it once and had been struck speechless at her strength. She turned her head from the pot she was stirring and saw Olan standing by the door.

He didn't dare step any farther into the kitchen until he was given permission. He had learned that a long time ago, and he didn't ever want to be yelled at like that ever again. The kitchen was Elsa's domain, and she had no problem with enforcing that fact on people.

"Is that you Olan?" she called.

He nodded.

"Come in, my boy. You are letting the heat out."

He closed the kitchen door behind him and made his way over to her, trying not to touch anything as he passed. "It smells good in here," he said as he reached her.

"Thank you. We are preparing the funeral feast for the late King," she explained. "So, what can I do for you, my boy?"

"I am here to get something for Lord Llywelyn for supper. He won't be joining the feast. He is very tired," Olan said, catching the eye of the same maid that had smiled at Llywelyn before and giving her a wink. She blushed and kept on cutting a large number of vegetables before her.

"That makes two of them now," she said. "Lord Owain is staying in his room tonight as well. I don't blame them. All the nobles from across the land are coming to the feast tonight."

"I shudder at the thought," Olan said, shaking his head.

"I know what you mean," she said.

"Oh, before I forget, Lord Llywelyn and I are going away for a trip into the countryside tomorrow, and so

I was wondering if you could spare some food for the journey?"

"Of course, how much do you need?"

"About three week's worth. If you can spare it."

"No problem." She turned her head to the young woman cutting the vegetables. "Talia, start putting together a package of food for Lord Llywelyn and young Olan here."

"Yes, mam," Talia said, putting down her knife and pulling down a tray from one of the sideboards and began filling it with foodstuffs.

"Don't forget some of the meat pies and some of the pastries as well," Elsa said, turning back to her kettle.

"Yes, mam," Talia said again, pulling down a loaf of bread and a jar of honey. The castle kept its own bees as well as a small number of fruit trees and a kitchen garden. Olan watched her as she filled the tray and marveled at her slender waist, and marveled at how her hair seemed to ripple as she moved like it had a life of its own.

"You like her don't you?" Elsa observed.

"What?" Olan said distractedly.

"Never mind," Elsa said with a smile.

Talia walked up to them with a tray full of food and handed it to Olan. He smiled at her, and she gave him a weak one back.

"Thank you very much," he said, giving her a small bow of the head.

"Stop that or I will hit you with my spoon," Elsa said, and taking down two wooden bowls filled them with stew, and added them to the tray. She placed two wooden spoons beside the bowls and made a shooing motion with her hands.

"Thank you so much, Elsa. This food will feed us like kings for weeks," he said.

"Good, now get out of my kitchen. I have a lot of work to do."

He nodded. Balancing the heavy tray carefully in both arms, he made his way back through the kitchen and out the door into the hall once more.

Llywelyn began packing some things they would need for their journey into a couple of saddlebags that had been laying against the wall. There were two more bags there beside the others, but they were reserved for the foodstuffs. As he packed, he thought about his grandfather. The man had been such an influence in his life. He had even been the one that had fought him in his final days of warrior training and gave him his very own sword to carry when he had completed his training.

He stood up and walked over to the table and sat down. He pulled open the drawer in the side of the table and took out parchment, quill, and ink, and began to write a quick note to his parents. As he wrote, he felt a single tear roll down his face, and fall off the tip of his nose onto the parchment, smearing the ink a little in his signature. He folded up the note. Closing up the ink well, he put it away again along with his quill.

Just then he heard a light knock at the bedroom door. He stood up and opened the door to find Olan standing there with the largest tray of food he had ever seen. He held the door open wide for him as he maneuvered the tray through the doorway and into the room and then closed the door once more. Olan walked over to the table and placed the tray gratefully on it.

"Are you sure you got enough Olan?" Llywelyn asked, laughing.

"I thought it was better to be safe than sorry," Olan said, picking up one of the bowls of stew, handing it and one of the spoons to Llywelyn. Llywelyn inhaled deeply and smiled.

"This smells delicious. Did Elsa make it?" he asked.

"The one and only," Olan replied, sitting down and dipping a spoon into his bowl of stew.

Llywelyn sat down on the bed and began to eat, savoring every bite as he put it in his mouth as if it was his last meal. "So what did you get?" he asked, lowering his spoon.

"I am not entirely sure. Talia piled the tray so high. But I know she gave some meat pies and a loaf of bread and some honey to go with it at least." Olan replied, scraping the bottom of his bowl for the last few chunks of meat.

"Great. We can pack it all in the last two saddlebags when we are finished," Llywelyn said, spooning more stew into his mouth. They finished consuming the meal in silence. When they finished, they both took a bag each, stuffing all the leftover food into them until they were bulging fit to burst with it all. Talia had even managed to put a couple of stone bottles of beer on the tray as well, explaining why the tray had been so heavy to carry.

"I should probably take the bowls and the tray back to the kitchen now, or Elsa will skin me alive and make me into stew next," Olan said, standing up.

"Good idea," Llywelyn said. "I don't think I would want to eat that."

"No, I wouldn't think so," Olan said, picking up the empty bowls and spoons. Olan left the room once more.

After he left, Llywelyn walked over to the bed and lay down on it. It had been a long hard day, and he was desperately tired from so much emotion. He closed his eyes, and within moments was fast asleep and didn't wake again until the next morning.

The next morning, Olan entered Llywelyn's room carrying a bowl of hot porridge to find him already up and dressed for travel. He saw Olan and smiled.

"Is that breakfast?" he asked.

"Yes, it is," Olan replied, handing him the bowl of porridge and a spoon.

"Fantastic. I'm starving," Llywelyn said, digging in. He ate the porridge with single-mindedness until there was nothing left in the bowl. Olan shook his head at him in amazement.

"Wow, you were hungry," he said.

"I told you," Llywelyn said with another smile. Olan took the empty bowl from him and put it on the table. That was when he saw the note sitting there.

"What's this?" he asked.

"It is a note for my parents. I am going to slip it under their door on the way," Llywelyn said, standing up and pulling on his traveling cloak and boots. Olan gave the bowl and spoon a quick rinse from a small basin that sat on the bedside table and then placed them both in the first of the four saddlebags. Llywelyn slipped the note into his cloak pocket. Picking up two of the saddlebags, he headed for the door. Olan picked up the second two bags and followed him out of the bedroom.

His parent's room was only a short distance down the hall from his own, and he quickly slipped the note under their door as they passed on their way out of the castle for them to find later. They made their way out of the castle, and through the courtyard in the direction of the stables.

The stables were dark as they entered, and the only sound was that of horses chewing hay. They found their horse stalls and began to saddle and bridle their horses before anyone in the castle realized they were leaving. They buckled the saddlebags onto their saddles, and mounting the horses, rode out of the stables into the bright dawn light.

They reached the castle gates and were waved through by the guard on morning duty. Once through the gates, they gave their horses a light kick and galloped off into the distance. Llywelyn felt completely carefree as he rode away from the castle and the town. Nothing and no one could keep him if he didn't want to stay. He was his own man, and he liked it that way. He felt relieved to know it was not he who would be taking on the task of ruling of Gwynedd in three days time.

Three days later, Dafydd, the elder, was crowned ruler of Wales. By this time, Llywelyn was far away in the Welsh countryside. The people of Gwynedd had yet to see what kind of a ruler Dafydd would become. Only time would show his true nature.

Chapter 3

The Danger Zone

Winchester Castle, Chester England, one month later…

King Henry III of England sat in the council chamber of Winchester Castle discussing the raids by the Welsh on the English border. The room was small, with a single long table, running the length of the room with a small fireplace at one end that cast shadows on the walls. Henry was a large man, with a pleasant round face, short brown hair, and close-set green eyes. He was known for his love of food and wine which gave him a rather pudgy look to his middle. He looked to his top general, Lord Edmond, and asked, “What information do you have on the raids in the north?” Lord Edmond was an uncommonly tall man and built like a tank. A wise and confident leader, men looked up to him and always tried to do their best. Now that the King was a little older and didn’t go to war as often; he left it to Lord Edmond to lead his soldiers into battle.

“The Welsh continue to be ruthless in their raiding on our soldiers. They come in the night and steal horses and supplies, and then they just disappear into the night like magic," Lord Edmond replied. This matter with the Welsh raiders stuck with him like a thorn in his side because he felt like he was letting his King down by not stopping it. But he didn't have the know-how. They were so fast and cunning that it didn't seem to matter what level of soldiers he placed at the northern border.

On the King's right sat Lord William, his lord regent who voiced his opinion on the matter. "Llywelyn the Great's work no doubt." Lord William was not only the King's Lord Regent, but he was also his long-time friend. They had grown up together, and he would do anything for his King. He would even go as far as to lay down his life for the man.

On the King's left sat Sir Stanley, his best knight. Sir Stanley was a tall man six feet even with his short curly black hair, and small dark-blue eyes that seemed to see straight through you when he looked at you. He was all muscle and had a large scar across one cheek from a battle many years before. He lived to fight and was a master the long sword and the bow.

"I don't know," Sir Stanley said. "It sounds more like his son Gruffudd. I have seen him leading battalions of Welsh soldiers across the border before."

"Have you fought them yourself?" Lord William asked.

"Yes, I have," Sir Stanley replied and shuttered at the memory.

Next to Lord Edmond sat another man, Lord Rosen, the Royal Treasurer. Lord Rosen was a small thin man with receding gray hair, powder-blue eyes, and a pale complexion from spending so much of his time indoors. Like the rest of the men at the table, all his attention was focused on Sir Stanley. "What are they like?" he asked.

"They are ruthless and skilled fighters. Especially, Lord Gruffudd," Sir Stanley replied.

"What level of soldiers are you leaving to guard the northern border Lord Edmond?" Lord William asked.

"They are perfectly competent soldiers," Lord Edmond said defensively. Lord Rosen smiled at his partner's defensiveness. He supposed it was second nature to a soldier, especially one as far up as him.

"If the Welsh are managing to steal their horses and supplies, then it sounds like there needs to be a higher level of soldiers guarding the northern border," Lord William said. The King nodded his head in approval and turned to Lord Rosen.

"Is this feasible Lord Rosen?" he asked.

"Yes, I think so," Lord Rosen replied. "It will just take some doing to find the funds. Though I think it is essential to deal with these Welsh raiders as soon as possible. Every time we lose a horse we are losing a valuable asset."

"See to the change in the border guards then Lord Edmond," the King said turning back to him. Lord Edmond nodded his head in acquiescence.

"Yes, Your Majesty," he said, and standing up he left the chamber.

Henry cleared his throat. "Well, that is taken care of at least," he said, settling himself more comfortably in his chair. Just then, there came a knock on the chamber door. "Enter," he called. The door opened, and a servant entered the room.

"Your Majesty, I have a message for you from Gwynedd, Wales," the servant said with a small bow.

"Bring it here then."

The man walked up to the King and placed the sealed message in his hand.

Henry broke the seal and began to read the message inside. He looked up from the message and saw the servant still standing there and cleared his throat once more.

"I think we need some wine," he said.

"Yes, right away, Your Majesty." The man turned then and left the chamber once more.

When the door had closed behind the servant, Sir Stanley cleared his throat to speak. "What does the message say, Your Majesty?" he asked.

"Llywelyn The Great has died," Henry said with a note of something like shock in his voice.

"Is that all it says?" Lord Rosen asked.

"No," Henry said. "His son Dafydd has taken over the rule of Gwynedd. He is calling himself Prince of Wales."

"This isn't good," Lord William said with a note of foreboding in his voice.

"What action should we take?" Lord Rosen asked. Just then, the door opened, and the servant entered the chamber carrying a flagon of wine and several cups that he placed on the table in front of the King, giving him a small bow.

"Thank you. You may go," Henry said, opening the wine. The servant nodded his head and left the chamber once more. Henry poured wine into three of the cups and handed one each to lords Rosen, and William, and Sir Stanley before pouring one for himself. He sat back in his chair and took a long swallow of wine, savoring the taste of it as it ran down his throat.

Following his lead, each of the men took a swallow from their own cups and then put them back on the table.

Lord William wiped his lips with the back of his sleeve and cleared his throat to speak. "I think you need to make a treaty with Lord Dafydd before it is too late," he said.

"I agree," Henry said, taking another sip of wine from his cup.

"I think Lord Gruffudd needs to be a part of this treaty as well," Lord William said, taking another sip of wine.

"Yes." Sir Stanley agreed. "He is much too powerful to stay at his brother's side."

"I will say that I will allow him to keep his land and his title on the condition that he sends me Lord Gruffudd in return," Henry said, taking yet another swallow of wine.

"Very good," Lord William said with a smile. "We can put him in The Tower of London to ensure he doesn't cause the crown any more trouble."

"Agreed," Henry said with a smile of his own.

"I will take the message to Gwynedd, Your Majesty," Sir Stanley offered. Henry smiled at him.

"If there was anyone I could trust to take my message to Gwynedd, it would be you. Please be careful. It may be dangerous, and I still need my best knight," he said.

"I will be careful," Sir Stanley promised. "I know what I am doing."

"All the same, you are heading into the Welsh stronghold," Lord William said with a note of concern in his voice.

"I am well aware that I am heading into the danger zone. But I assure you that I will be on my guard at all times," Sir Stanley said with what he hoped was a reassuring smile.

Henry placed his now empty cup on the table and wiped his lips with the back of his sleeve. "On that note, let us retire to the dining hall. I'm starved," he said.

The men nodded their heads in agreement, and they all stood up and left the chamber.

The next morning, Sir Stanley rode out of the gates of Winchester Castle and started on the road to Gwynedd, Wales. The sun was bright, and there wasn't a single cloud in the sky. It was a good omen for his journey.

Lord William watched him go with a worried look on his face. Sir Stanley had been a good friend for many years, and he was concerned about the man riding into enemy territory alone. Yes, Sir Stanley was a very talented fighter, but so were the kinds of people Stanley would soon be facing. He watched until his friend was out of sight and then turned and walked back into the castle.

The road to Gwynedd was a long one. Each night Sir Stanley would set up a small camp in the woods and feed his horse, and then himself. Each night before he slept, he would check to make sure he still had the papers for the treaty in his pocket. He didn't mind sleeping in the woods. He liked the sounds of the woods at night. He found it soothing to listen to. The air was also a lot cleaner out here in the forest than it was in the confines of the castle with all the smoke from the many fires that warmed each and every chamber in the place as well as the almost constant haze of pipe smoke. He didn't smoke himself, but several of the men he knew did including the King himself. Quite often he would escape to the stables to breathe in the smells of the animals that smelled much better to him than that of dirty wet laundry that regularly permeated the various bed chambers.

"How do you like this I wonder?" he asked his horse one evening as he gave her a rub down after the day's riding. "It must be nice for you to be out in the fresh air for a change." The horse blew softly in his face and bumped her head into his shoulder. He laughed and patted her on the withers. He turned then and went to check on his supper. Finding the stew ready to eat, he poured it into a wooden bowl he had brought with him in one of his saddlebags and sat down on the ground by the fire to eat it. It was early spring, and the ground was covered in a layer of short course grass which his horse happily chewed away at. He wondered what kind of reception he could expect at Lord Dafydd's castle. He wondered if Lord Gruffudd would be there as well. He hoped Lord Gruffudd wouldn't be, because it would be very awkward seeming the man was a part of the treaty between the two kingdoms.

After he had finished eating, he poured a small amount of water into the bowl to rinse it before placing it back in the saddlebag. Then he pulled out his blanket and lay down on the ground to sleep. As he lay on his back looking up at the stars, he thought he could almost see a part of a constellation, but he couldn't be sure. Being a knight he was a very light sleeper in general. He had learned early on to never fall in too deep asleep, so that he could always stay alert in case of trouble. It enabled him to snap to attention in a matter of seconds, and this ability had saved his life on more than one occasion over the years. He took a few deep breaths and tried to clear his mind of thought in order to sleep. He closed his eyes and was asleep within moments.

About three weeks after leaving Winchester Castle, he finely reached the northern border between England and Gwynedd, Wales. He rode into a small clearing, and dismounted, and began his usual camp routine as he had done for the past three weeks. He whistled under his breath as he built the fire and began cooking his evening meal. He had felt a sense of relief when he had seen that he had finally reached the border between his homeland and the unknown land of Gwynedd, Wales. So far it had been an uneventful trip, and he felt confident that he could pull off this mission without any problems. He checked his pocket once more and found that the papers were still there—a little crumpled maybe, but intact all the same. After supper, he fell fast asleep without any difficulty, and without a single thought in his mind. Everything was all right.

His first indication of trouble was his horse. She was normally very quiet at night. He came awake to the sound of her stomping her hooves and snorting in agitation. He looked over at her and in the light from the dying fire he could see her nostrils flared in alarm. At first, he thought it might be some kind of wild animal that was scaring her and looked around for any sign of something hiding in the trees. But he didn't see anything. He was about to lie down again and try to get back to sleep when he heard a sound that no animal would ever make. It was so faint that it was almost imperceptible, but he knew right away what it was, and in the silence of the woods, it seemed to ring out clear as a bell. The sound of chainmail clinking: it sounded like several men were changing position back in the deep shadows of the trees that surrounded his clearing.

He rolled out of his blankets and crawled over to where he had left his saddlebags and his sword. He pulled his bow and an arrow out of one of the bags, and picking up his sword, removed it from its scabbard. He crawled back to his blankets, and crouching down, knocked the arrow to the bowstring. He put the bow to his shoulder and pulling the string back to his cheek, let the arrow fly into the trees beyond.

There was a moment of complete silence, and then all hell broke loose. He jumped to his feet, wielding his sword as about what looked like at least a dozen Welshmen burst out of the trees wielding weapons of their own. Some had swords while others held what looked like clubs. Two men caught his attention. They both held axes and they were running straight towards him with the look of murder in their eyes. As the group of Welshmen ran towards him, they were yelling something that sounded like some kind of war cry, but it was in Welsh. He couldn't understand a word of it. He did understand one thing though. These men meant to kill him and take everything he had, including his horse.

He raised his sword high and charged at the men with a yell. They seemed to come at him from all sides.

He swung his sword expertly and tried his best to meet each attacker; however, it was far from easy. He would kill one man only to find yet another blade coming at him from the other side. He deflected the new blade with a backward swing. Another man tried to stab him from behind. His horse was screaming in fright now, and tried to break her hobbles. He prayed that they would hold as he fought even harder. He knew that if he managed to beat these men, he would need her to make a quick getaway before even more men showed up.

Soon, after what felt like an eternity, there were only three men left standing. The rest were either dead or too injured to fight anymore. Panting from the effort of the fight, he turned his sword on the first of the three men.

"Yield," he said, staring into the man's eyes, which were a deep rich brown that almost looked black in the dim light from the dying fire. The man glared back at him in defiance.

"In your dreams," the man growled and swung his sword at Sir Stanley's head. He ducked and stabbed the man in the chest with his blade. Lucky for him the man had only been wearing padded leather and not chainmail, so his sword went in easily. The man fell silently to the ground, dead. As the man fell, Sir Stanley released his sword, and with his bloody sword held high, he turned to face the second man.

"Yield," he demanded. The man glared at him with such hatred that he almost took a step backward. But he held his ground and stared back at the man in turn.

"Never," said the man shaking his head.

"Will you give up this pointless self-destruction or die like the rest of them?" Sir Stanley asked almost lazily.

"We will never bow down to English rule," the man said defiantly. "Go back to your King and tell him so like a good little servant," Sir Stanley smiled.

"Now it is you who is dreaming," he said. Both men swung their swords at the same time, their blades met with the ringing of metal on metal. After a short and ferocious engagement, Sir Stanley killed the man with a stab to the heart. He turned his back on the man as he fell and saw the last man left standing: he was staring straight into the face of Llywelyn ap Gruffudd. As he looked into his face, he felt goose bumps run up his spine. There was something about him that made him feel like he was in the presence of a King. He may only have been 17 or 18, but he had an air of command and power to him not unlike how he felt when he was with King Henry. Llywelyn looked into Sir Stanley's eyes as he lowered his sword in surrender, and Sir Stanley did the same without thinking. His blood was pulsing in his veins with adrenalin and he could feel his arms and legs shaking. He was not as young as he once had been, and his years were catching up with him. But this was not the time to show weakness.

"I yield," Llywelyn said and dropped his sword on the ground at his feet.

"You are an intelligent man," Sir Stanley observed. Llywelyn shook his head.

"You have either killed or injured every one of my men," he said. "I would be a fool to throw away the only life I have here with you, and I am no fool."

"No, you don't strike me as a foolish man. Brave perhaps, but not foolish," Sir Stanley said with a smile.

"You are very perceptive for an Englishman."

"Have you met many?" Sir Stanley asked amused.

"Enough," Llywelyn replied. Sir Stanley was surprised at how easy it was to talk to the man.

"What is your name?" he asked eager to know who he was.

"I am Llywelyn ap Gruffudd. The grandson of the late Llywelyn, The Great of Gwynedd Wales," Llywelyn said with a note of pride in his voice.

Sir Stanley held out his hand, and Llywelyn took it briefly."I am Sir Stanley, and I am bound to deliver a message to your Prince from King Henry of England," he said.

Llywelyn shook his head. "He is not my Prince."

"But I thought that Dafydd ap Llywelyn was calling himself Prince of Wales?" Sir Stanley said confused.

"He is," Llywelyn confirmed. "But he is not my Prince."

"I'm sorry, I misspoke," Sir Stanley said apologetically.

"That is a nice-looking horse you have here," Llywelyn said changing the subject.

"Yes, she is a good one," Sir Stanley agreed.

"Yes, I can see that," Llywelyn said with a nod.

"Why did you really yield to me?" Sir Stanley asked.

"I told you; I value my life," Llywelyn said adjusting his armor slightly. He had been one of the men that had been wearing chainmail, and he was desperate to take it off. It was very heavy.

"I see," Sir Stanley said still not trusting that he was getting the whole truth. Llywelyn focused his gaze on Sir Stanley's face and continued.

"But there is one thing that you should know," he said.

"And what is that then?" Sir Stanley asked.

"I never forget a face," Llywelyn said.

"What is that supposed to mean?"

"As much as I value my life, yours I do not," Llywelyn said. "All these men that were here with me tonight were simply out for sport. They were not skilled fighters and that is why you were able to defeat them so easily. They were not warriors, but I am and if I ever see you again I will kill you, and I will do it without a second thought." Llywelyn gave a short whistle, and his horse came trotting out of the trees and stopped beside him. He mounted up and galloped off into the night.

Sir Stanley stood in the clearing among the dead and dying and watched him ride away with a mixture of relief and curiosity. He had said that he was the son of Lord Gruffudd and the grandson of Llywelyn, The Great, and he believed him. The way he had handled his blade had reminded him vividly of Lord Gruffudd. He had also seen the look in his eyes when he had said those final words. He meant what he had said, and Sir Stanley had no doubt in his mind that if he ever saw the young man again he would be a dead man.

Feeling like he had narrowly escaped death himself, he quickly gathered up his things and saddled his horse. Then he mounted up and rode out of the clearing to find another place to sleep until dawn. If he could sleep that was. His heart was still racing with adrenalin and he couldn't get Llywelyn's final words out of his mind or the look on his face. Lord William had been worried about Lord Gruffudd, but it was clear to Sir Stanley that Gruffudd's son was the one to be watched. It was clear to him that he didn't truly have any idea about the kinds of dangers he could be facing on this mission, and that he truly didn't understand anything about the way these people worked.

Chapter 4

The King's Messenger

The next morning dawned warm and bright as Sir Stanley struck camp, and after checking to make sure he still had the papers, he saddled his horse and rode out of the clearing. He crossed the border into Gwynedd a few hours later and started on the road to Aberfraw Castle in the Clwyd Valley. He was constantly on the lookout for danger as he rode now that he was in enemy territory, but he didn't see anyone on the road. But it didn't stop him from looking over his shoulder every few minutes as he rode, and he kept his bow and arrows and his sword by his side at night and slept very lightly, always listening for the slightest sound that may indicate some sort of trouble.

It was another week before he reached the outskirts of the village and town that surrounded Aberfraw Castle. He was surprised to see such a thriving place in such a barbaric land. Small stone cottages that housed the farmers and their families populated the village landscape. Women sat in groups outside talking to one another and mending torn clothes or washing laundry in a communal barrel.

Small children in grubby clothing ran barefoot amongst the vegetables while their men worked the fields and tended to the livestock that supplied the town and the castle's inhabitance with food. The children stared at him while he rode through their midst and pointed at him while babbling in their strange language. He wished he knew what they were saying, but their words were lost on him. They didn't seem hostile though, just curious of this stranger riding through their village. He must look very strange to them he thought. He doubted any of these people had ever seen an Englishman before in their lives.

As he rode into the town, he began to see much larger buildings. The place was filled with people coming and going, and they were all chatting away in the same unintelligible language of the land. He noticed that while it was a fairly guttural language, it almost had a singsong quality to it as well. In the town square, there were several stalls set up with people selling their wares. They called out to him as he rode past; they tried to wave him over, but he ignored them and kept moving through the crowded streets. He made his way ever closer to his destination.

He saw several houses and what looked like an inn as well as what seemed to be a tavern. The entire town was dominated by the castle that stood on top of a hill in the distance. From here, he could see its towers, but not its gate. It looked formidable to him even from a distance and made him feel a little nervous just looking at it. One would have to be a complete fool to even consider trying to storm the place.

As he rode down the short road from the town to the castle and up the hill, he found that the building seemed to loom over him more and more the closer he got to it. He could now see the large metal gate and what looked like a guard tower on the wall beside the gate. Now he felt very nervous and was starting to second guess the entire mission. The guards in the gate tower saw him coming and hailed him as he reached the castle gate.

"Stop where you are sir, and state your purpose," the first of the two guards said. He was burly looking man with short curly blond hair and a mustache made his face look rather severe. The man was very intimidating even at this distance as he stared into the knight's face with his close-set brown eyes without blinking. Sir Stanley sat straight in his saddle and met the man's gaze straight on.

"My name is Sir Stanley, and I have come to deliver a message to Lord Dafydd from King Henry III of England," he replied. The second guard was staring at him now as well. He had shoulder-length, copper-colored hair, and his face was bare of any facial hair. He looked interestedly at Sir Stanley with small beady amber-colored eyes that seemed to be sizing him up.

"What kind of message would the King of England have for our Prince?" the man asked in a deep voice that sent shivers up his spine.

"I am sorry, but I am not permitted to discuss it with anyone other than the Prince himself," Sir Stanley replied. He watched as the two men put their heads together for a moment or two before turning back to him once more.

"You may enter," the blond-haired guard said; stepping down off the guard tower, he opened a large metal gate with a grinding of hinges and waved Sir Stanley through into the courtyard beyond.

He dismounted and turned to the two guards.

"It has been a long journey, and my horse will need food and water," he said.

"Of course," the second guard said. "You may leave her here, and one of the stable boys will come and take care of her."

"Thank you," Sir Stanley said. Giving his horse a quick pat on the shoulder, he turned and walked towards the front doors of the castle which were held open by the guard Cammo. He smiled at the man and walked through the doors and into the front hall beyond.

A servant in a light green wool shirt and leggings walked up to him as he stood in the front hall. The man had a small triangular face and large almost yellow eyes and short-cropped tan hair. He gave Sir Stanley a small bow of the head and a small smile. The man's smile made him feel much better. Here in the castle, there was at least one civil person.

"Can I help you?" the man asked, staring at him with open curiosity.

"My name is Sir Stanley, and I am here to deliver a message to Lord Dafydd from King Henry III of England," he said with what he hoped was a reassuring smile.

The man returned his smile. "Well, he is a bit busy at the moment," the man said. "But I can tell him that you are here."

"I have had a long journey. Is there somewhere I could sit down to wait?" Sir Stanley asked, suddenly feeling very tired.

"Yes, of course. Right this way." The man led him around the corner and into a small alcove that was closed off by a curtain and contained a single chair which he sank into gratefully.

"Thank you," he said.

"I will go and tell his Grace that you are here," the man said, and with another bow of the head, he left Sir Stanley alone to wait.

Meanwhile, Dafydd sat in the great hall eating lunch and looking over a list of complaints from the people in the town and the village beyond. Many of the complaints seemed to be of a similar nature.

Sanena sat across from him, drinking brandy and staring into space. She was worried about her son, Llywelyn and the stress had her stomach in knots, making it impossible for her to eat. Her cup slipped out of her hand and fell to the stone floor with a smash, soaking her skirt and the table cloth with brandy. Dafydd managed to pick up his papers just in time before they were damaged and glared at her.

"Jesus Sanena, what did you do that for?" he demanded angrily.

"Sorry, My Lord," she mumbled, looking at her hands.

"My Prince," he corrected.

"Of course," she said, raising her face to look at him. "How could I forget? Please, forgive my mistake, My Prince." She smiled at him and gave a small bow of the head.

"Oh, how hollow your words sound," he said. "It is almost like you don't believe them."

"I don't know what you are talking about?" she said, shaking her head.

"No?" he said with a smile of his own.

"No," she said. He shook his head, and picking up his cup of brandy, took a sip.

"Do you know where your son is?" he asked, putting the cup back on the table.

"Which one?" she asked. "I have four."

"Llywelyn," Dafydd said with a note of humor in his voice. "Do you know where he is?"

"No, I don't," she said honestly. "Llywelyn left a note saying he was going away for a while to deal with his grief. But he didn't say anything about where he was going or how long he would be gone."

"I see," Dafydd said. Just then there came a knock on the hall door. "Come in," he called. The door opened and the servant who had greeted Sir Stanley entered the hall. He walked to Dafydd and gave him a small bow.

"My Prince, there is someone here to see you," he said.

"Did they give their name?" Dafydd asked.

"Yes, My Prince," the man said, giving another bow of the head. "He said that his name was Sir Stanley and that he has a message for you from the King of England." This turn of events was unexpected. He wondered what kind of message the King of England would want to give him badly enough that he would send a knight to deliver it and not just some lowly servant. He made a great effort to gather his thoughts and turned to the man.

"You can tell him that I will speak with him," he said. The man nodded and left the hall.

"I wonder what that is all about?" Sanena said after the door had closed. Dafydd drained his cup and picking the decanter, refilled it once more, and took a sip. Then he put the cup back on the table and looked at his erstwhile sister-in-law.

"I don't know," he said. "But in any case, it doesn't concern you."

She shook her head.

"I am the wife of your head warrior and brother," she reminded him.

"Just being the wife of my brother Gruffudd doesn't give you any privileges here," he said. "It would be good for you to remember that from now on."

She rolled her eyes in exasperation.

He had tried to pull this kind of thing on her before over the years. While his father had been alive, he had always come to her aid, but now the man was gone. But Dafydd was the ruler now, and since he had taken the crown things had seemed to get a lot worse between them.

"And you think being my brother-in-law gives you any?" she scoffed.

"I am Your Prince," he said. "I think that says it all don't you?"

"You may be the ruler of Gwynedd, Dafydd," she agreed. "But you will be my Prince the day hell freezes over."

He glared at her with open dislike. "Get out," he snarled.

She shrugged and stood up to leave. "Fine, I will go," she said. "Good luck dealing with the machinations of the English King." She gave him a dirty look and stocked out of the hall, slamming the door behind her as she left.

Dafydd sighed and picked up his cup, draining it in one. Then he picked up his papers once more and went back to reading. After a minute or so, he gave it up and put them back down again. He couldn't concentrate because his mind was too preoccupied with thoughts about his sister-in-law. It was no secret that they didn't like one another. He had never really forgiven his brother for marrying her in the first place. Even though her father Caradog had been a nobleman, he had still always thought Gruffudd could have done better. Caradog had been a lower-level noble, so hadn't had much for her dowry, and in the world of the royals' dowry was very important when it came to marriage. Gruffudd had fallen head over heels for her though and so had his parents, and thoughts he had on the matter had been thrown to the wayside. Then about a year after they had been married, Owain had been born and Llywelyn a couple of years after that and it became clear that she was here for good.

Llywelyn resembled his father in many ways, but he looked an awful like his grandfather as well. He was strong like his grandfather, and he had the same air of command about him that Dafydd himself had never himself. It could be a little unsettling sometimes to see just how alike they truly were.

A knock on the hall door pulled him out of his thoughts.

"Come in," he called. The door opened, and the servant entered the hall, followed closely by Sir Stanley. He led him up to the table, and when he reached Dafydd, gave him a small bow.

"My Prince, let me introduce Sir Stanley," he said. Dafydd smiled at the man.

"Thank you, Huw. You may go now," Dafydd said. The servant gave him another small bow and left the hall once more. He turned then to Sir Stanley and smiled at him in greeting. Sir Stanley gave a small bow of the head and returned the smile.

"Won't you take a seat?" Dafydd said, pointing to the chair across the table that Sanena had recently vacated. Sir Stanley nodded and walked over to the chair and sat down in it facing him.

"Thank you for agreeing to see me," Sir Stanley said.

"Not at all," Dafydd said. "Would you like some brandy?"

"Yes, please," Sir Stanley said eagerly. He hadn't had anything to drink for a while and he was parched.

Dafydd picked up the decanter and poured brandy into a cup and passed it to Sir Stanley. He took the cup with a nod of thanks and took a large sip, enjoying the taste of the brandy as it trickled down his throat.

"This is excellent brandy," he observed.

"Yes, it is some of our best," Dafydd agreed, taking a sip of his own. "My servant tells me that you have a message for me from the King of England?"

"Yes, I do," Sir Stanley said sitting up straighter in his chair and placing his cup back on the table.

"What message does the King have for me then?" Dafydd asked, putting his cup back on the table as well.

Sir Stanley undid the clasp of his traveling cloak and removing it. He hung the cloak over the back of his chair. Then he settled himself more comfortably and cleared his throat. "The King feels that there has been fighting between our two lands for far too long now," he said, picking up his cup, and taking another sip of brandy.

Dafydd nodded his head in agreement. "I see," he said. "And what does the King propose to do about it?"

"He has sent me here with a treaty for you to sign that will ensure peace between us," Sir Stanley said, taking another sip from his cup.

Dafydd smiled to himself. He should have expected something like this.

"And what is in it for me?" he asked.

"The King will allow you to keep your land and your title," Sir Stanley replied.

The amusement Dafydd had felt a second before now changed to hot anger at the King's presumption. He didn't own Wales, and therefore could not let Dafydd keep it like he was offering him a present, and as for his title, well, that was out of his hands as well. But why not play along with it a little more? This man had come an awful long way to tell him such ridiculousness after all, and what kind of host would he be to just turn him away so quickly. "What does the King intend to do if I do not comply with his wishes?" he asked.

"He will start a war between us to decide things once and for all," Sir Stanley said bluntly.

"I see." He did see. This attitude was how such men thought after all. They would use bribes and threats to get what they wanted no matter the consequences.

"What are his terms?" he asked.

"In return for peace between the two lands, he requests that you send him your head warrior, Gruffudd," Sir Stanley replied.

"What will happen to him if I send him to the King?"

"He will be placed in The Tower of London to ensure he doesn't cause the crown any more trouble."

"I see," Dafydd said, picking up his cup and taking a long swallow of brandy. Then he put the cup back on the table and wiped his lips with the back of his hand. "I will need some time to think this over," he said.

"I understand," Sir Stanley said. "I will return here tomorrow morning before I leave for England. You have until then to make your decision." He stood up then, and throwing his cloak back around his shoulders, turned to leave.

"You are welcome to stay here in the castle. I will have a room prepared for you," Dafydd offered.

"No, thank you," Sir Stanley said. "I saw a respectable looking inn in the town, and I will stay there for the night." He turned then and left the hall.

Dafydd remained at the table by himself for a few minutes after the man had left, drinking his brandy, and thinking over the King's request. Then, he stood up and left the hall for his room. He didn't know what to think. He felt like a fly caught in a spider web, but he couldn't see the strands, and that unnerved him no end. He had only been the ruler of Gwynedd for a little over two months, and it was already turning out to be more than he could handle. He didn't know how his father had done it. He wished more than ever that he could talk to him and ask him what he should do. He felt lost and alone and a little scared.

Sir Stanley retrieved his horse, and he rode out of the castle gate and back down the road towards the town.

Once he had re-entered the town, he managed to find the inn again fairly quickly and headed straight for it. He wanted nothing more at that moment than a warm meal and a good night's sleep in a soft bed before starting back on the road to England once more. When he reached the inn, he dismounted and tied his horse to the doorpost before pushing the door open and going inside.

The front room was spacious and filled with a haze of pipe smoke. He could see several men sucking on the end of pipes filled with some sort of grassy substance. In the corner of the room, a roaring fire cast light over the tables filled with people eating and drinking. Near the door stood the bar with a door behind it, which he assumed must lead to the kitchens beyond. On the far side of the room, a set of rickety wooden stairs led to the upper levels where the rooms would be.

He could smell the tantalizing aroma of roasting meat mingled with the smell of the pipe smoke and ale. He smiled at the smells and walked up to the bar. He smiled at the bartender with what he hoped was a reassuring smile. The man was short with straw-like graying hair, small light gray eyes set into a small round face. The man had the kind of face that always seemed to be smiling even when he wasn't.

The man said something in Welsh, pointing at Sir Stanley. He shook his head in incomprehension.

"English, do you speak English?" he asked desperately. The man smiled at him and nodded once.

"You come to a new land without first learning the language? You must be very brave," the man observed.

"I am not here out of choice," Sir Stanley said. "I am here on business."

"Ah, business," the man said with a chuckle. "What can I do for you?"

"I need a room for the night and a hot meal," Sir Stanley said. "Also, I have a horse that will need a place to stay for the night as well as some food and water if you can provide it."

"It will cost you," the man said with another smile.

"I have silver. Name your price," Sir Stanley said, pulling out his purse. At the sight of the purse, the man's smile grew a little wider. Sir Stanley took out a silver coin and laid it on the counter.

"Three," the man said.

Sir Stanley shook his head, and reaching his purse, pulled out a second coin and placed it on the bar next to the first.

"The first is for a meal and a bed for the night, the second to take care of my horse. These are is silver after all. You don't mean to tell me you normally charge your customer's three silver pieces for a meal and a bed for the night, do you?"

The man laughed. "Two silver coins it is then," the man said, picking them up off the counter and pocketing them before turning and disappearing through the door into the kitchen beyond.

Sir Stanley made his way to the only empty table and sat down. He felt very uneasy sitting alone in this bar full of people who were staring at him with looks ranging from simple curiosity to outright hostility. He would feel much better tomorrow when he was back on the road to

England once more. For now, he tried to ignore the stares and to focus on his meeting in the morning with Lord Dafydd. The man was not what he had expected. He was nothing like his nephew Llywelyn, and he had seemed very uneasy talking to him. Almost, like he didn't have any confidence in himself as a ruler. But that was crazy. He would have known his father would die one day and must have been learning all he could from the man for many years. But still, he did seem very nervous when they were speaking. He wondered if he could use that to his advantage in some way.

A young woman with copper-colored hair that seemed to flow down the back of her brown homespun dress was making her way through the crowded room towards his table. As she walked, the men hooted and hollered at her in Welsh. He could see that she was used to them though because she simply smiled and flicked her hand at the men as she passed. She stopped at his table and smiled at him in welcome. He could see that she had the most beautiful hazel eyes with long lashes that seemed to dominate her small pretty face. She placed a wooden bowl full of steaming stew in front of him, and beside it, she placed a large pottery mug of ale. She gave him another smile and walked away.

"Wait," he said as she turned to go. "What is your name?" she said nothing and gave him another smile before walking away and disappearing through the kitchen door. He realized then that she must not have been able to speak English. He shrugged, picking up the wooden spoon that had been provided with his meal dipped into his bowl, and began to eat.

After he had finished his stew and drank his ale, he stood up and walked back to the bar to retrieve his key.

"Was your meal all right?" the man asked.

"It was very tasty thank you, and the ale was excellent," Sir Stanley said. The man handed him his key and he walked off towards the stairs. He walked up the short flight to the upper floor, finding his room, unlocked it, and went inside. He closed the door behind him and locked it for good measure. He didn't want anyone coming up here and surprising him in the night. The room was small with a single bed frame in the middle, and one shutterless window looking out at the town below, and a small fireplace which was cold. He didn't mind though. He just wanted to lie down and not get up again until the next morning. He was dead tired and could feel sleep pulling at him even as he took off his cloak and boots. He would sleep in his clothing though. He didn't know how clean the sheets were and he wasn't about to risk it. He climbed beneath the blankets and the moment his head hit the pillow he fell fast asleep and didn't wake again until the following morning.

Chapter 5

Arrest

Sir Stanley woke the next morning, and putting on his cloak and boots left his room, went back downstairs. The front room was quiet this early in the day. He placed his key back on the counter and left the inn to fetch his horse. He would have breakfast with Lord Dafydd up at the castle. He still couldn't think of Dafydd as a Prince somehow. Now Llywelyn on the other hand, well he radiated that sense of command and self-confidence that Sir Stanley had come to feel was a part of what made a great ruler. It was something that Lord Dafydd just seemed to be lacking which made it impossible for Sir Stanley to take him seriously as someone that demanded the title of Prince.

He collected his horse from the stable at the back of the inn and rode out of the town back towards the castle. When he reached the castle, the same blond guard from the day before opened the gate open for him once more.

"Nice day," the guard commented. There wasn't a cloud in the sky and the sun was out.

"Yes," Sir Stanley agreed and rode through the gate into the courtyard beyond. He dismounted and left his horse to be tended to like he had the day before and walked up to the front doors, which were opened for him by the guard Cammo once more who gave him a nod of greeting. He nodded back and walked through the doors into the front hall. The servant who had greeted him the day before, whose name he didn't know was waiting for him and led him to the great hall.

"His Grace is expecting you," the man said. He knocked once on the hall door, and when he heard the command to enter he opened the door and went inside, followed closely by Sir Stanley.

"Ah, Sir Stanley, it is good to see you again," Dafydd said as Sir Stanley walked up to the table where he sat eating breakfast.

"Yes," he agreed. He walked around the table and sat down in the same chair he had occupied the day before.

"Huw, bring some of the sweet wine," Dafydd said turning to the servant. Huw nodded and left the hall. "Sausages?" he asked.

"Yes, please," Sir Stanley said feeling his stomach rumble in anticipation. He always woke up hungry in the morning. Dafydd passed him the plate of sausages and he took three sausages from it and put them on a small plate. He picked up one of the sausages and took a bite. Immediately his mouth was flooded with saliva from the spicy taste of the meat. He chewed it slowly, savoring the taste before swallowing.

"These are delicious. You must give your cook my appreciation," he said taking another bite of sausage.

"I will do that. I am sure she will appreciate the compliment," Dafydd said taking a bite of bread. Just then the door opened again, and the servant, Huw walked up to the table carrying a flagon of sweet wine and two cups which he placed on the table in front of Dafydd with a small bow of the head.

"Thank you, Huw. You may go now," Dafydd said. Huw nodded and left the hall once more. "Wine?"

"Yes, please," Dafydd poured a measure of the wine into the two cups and handed one to Sir Stanley before taking a sip from his cup. Sir Stanley took a large sip of the wine and smiled at the taste.

"Very good," he said wiping his lips with the back of his hand.

"I am glad you like it," Dafydd said taking another sip of the wine. They sat for a time drinking wine and eating through some more of the sausages as well as some fruit and bread. After Sir Stanley had eaten his fill he sat back in his chair and cleared his throat to speak.

"Have you made a decision?" he asked.

"Yes, I have," Dafydd replied and took a large swallow of wine from his cup.

"And what have you decided?" Dafydd wiped his lips with his sleeve and placed his cup back on the table.

"I agree to the King's terms," he said.

"That is good to hear," Sir Stanley said surprised.

"But on one condition." There it was. Of course, the man would have conditions of his own.

"And what would that condition be?" he asked.

"I will send Lord Gruffudd to England," Dafydd agreed. "But on the condition that the King takes his son

Owain as well." Sir Stanley drained his cup of wine and placed the empty cup back on the table.

"What is this Owain to you?" he asked.

"He has been the strategist for the royal army for the past couple of years, but I have grown to have doubts about his loyalty to me. I am concerned he might be up to something like some kind of plot to overthrow me as ruler of Gwynedd." This was true enough. He knew there was no love lost between himself and his nephew, and he knew that the man would do anything to have his father ruler here or at least his brother Llywelyn.

"Well, I am sure that won't be a problem," Sir Stanley said.

"Then it is settled," Dafydd said and drained his cup in one swallow.

"Yes, I believe so," Sir Stanley agreed, and reaching into the pocket of his traveling cloak pulled out the papers that he had been carrying for the past several weeks and placed them on the table between them. On the table sat a small pottery jar full of quills and an iron ink well. Dafydd uncorked the inkwell and trimmed one of the quills to his liking while Sir Stanley laid out the treaty papers. Dafydd dipped the freshly trimmed quill into the ink and signed his name on several different points on the papers as Sir Stanley pointed them out. Then he recorked the inkwell and lay down his quill and smiled.

"Well, that is done now. Will you stay a little longer before you go? It is not often we get foreign visitors such as yourself here," he said.

"No, I really should start on the road as soon as possible so I can get a good amount of distance in before nightfall," Sir Stanley said.

Dafydd nodded in understanding. He stood up then, and walked to the hall door and opening it called out for the servant Huw. The man was not far away and came running to the door.

"Yes, My Prince?"

"I need you to bring me, two guards, as quickly as possible," Dafydd said. Huw nodded.

"Right away, My Prince," he said and hurried off to find the guards.

Dafydd closed the door again and walked back to the table to find Sir Stanley fastening his traveling cloak around his shoulders.

"I wish you a safe journey," he said.

"Thank you," Sir Stanley said and bowing left the hall. Dafydd sat back down at the table and refilled his cup with wine and waited for Huw to return with the two guards while he thought about the King's messenger and the treaty he had just agreed to sign.

Sir Stanley left the castle and retrieving his horse rode out of the gate and back down the road away from Aberfraw Castle with a feeling of relief. He rode back through the town and the village beyond all the while ignoring the stares of the people. Soon he would be back on the open road and away from them all. He felt much safer alone in the woods than he did among these strangers that spoke in such an alien tongue. A few more days and he would be back on English soil and on the road back to Winchester Castle where he felt truly safe.

Twenty minutes later, Dafydd was still sitting in the great hall drinking wine and thinking over the meeting he had just had with Sir Stanley when a knock came on the hall door.

"Come in," he called. The door opened, and two guards entered the hall. They walked up to the table where he sat and gave him a small bow. They were both muscular men of a similar height. Being brothers they had the same short brown hair and wide emerald green eyes set on either side of small snubbed noses.

"My Prince?" Royal, the elder of the two brothers said with another small bow.

"Jefferies, Royal, I need you to find Lord Owain and arrest him," Dafydd instructed. The two men nodded their heads in understanding.

"Yes, My Prince," Royal said.

"Where do you want us to take him?" Jefferies, the younger of the two asked.

"Take him into the town and place him in the town jail until he can be transported to England," Dafydd said.

"Yes, My Prince," the two brothers said as one and turning left the hall once more.

Owain sat in his room next to the fire reading from a book when there came a knock on the door.

"Come in," he called closing the book and placing it on the floor next to his chair. The door opened, and the two guards entered the room together. Owain was surprised to see them here, but not unhappy about it either. He had always liked the brothers. They closed the door and gave Owain a small bow. "Jefferies, Royal, what are you doing here?"

"We are here because the Prince has ordered us to arrest you," Royal said not looking at him.

Owain smiled at the two men. This had to be a joke of some kind surely. "You are hilarious," he said with a grin. "Now what is the real reason you are here?"

"He isn't joking, My Lord," Jefferies said. "We really are here because the Prince to has sent us here to arrest you."

"Well, you can tell him that I am not going anywhere," Owain said methodically clenching and unclenching his fists. "I am the son of Lord Gruffudd, and I will not be treated with such open disrespect. I demand to know the truth of what he is about because I can assure you he has told you nothing."

Royal shook his head. "We don't know what he is about this is true," he said.

"Ah ha, I told you," Owain said with a smile.

"It doesn't really matter one way or the other," Jefferies said.

"Of course it matters," Owain said.

"No, it doesn't," Royal said. "We were sent here to do a job and we intend to see it through. Now you can either come quietly or we can force you, but either way, you will be coming with us."

Owain smiled at these men's presumption that they could order a member of the royal family around like this. If he didn't want to go then he would not go, no matter if his uncle had ordered his removal from the castle or not.

"Well?" Jefferies said.

Owain smiled again and standing up to his full height squared his shoulders. At six feet he seemed to tower over the much shorter men, but there were two of them and only one of him. He may have been better with a sword than these two, but Llywelyn was the one who had always been better at close contact fighting without any sort of weapon other than his fists. But they would take him over his dead body. He would not give Dafydd the satisfaction of letting them take him without a fight.

He took a deep breath in and let it out again, and on the out-breath he took a swing from his hip and punched Royal in the chest, sending him flying backward into the door where he landed heavily with a loud thud.

Jefferies swung at him in turn, and a brief but intense fight ensued between the three men.

Owain fought valiantly, but in the end, he was no match for the two men. They were much better trained at hand-to-hand combat than he was, and so they were able to wear him down fairly easily. Once they had done so they placed a pair of metal handcuffs on his wrists, and marched him out of the room holding on to him by the upper arms. They marched him through the hallways to the front doors which were opened by a different guard and out into the weak sunlight of the courtyard beyond. Owain could see a small windowless carriage in the middle of the courtyard with two horses already harnessed to the front of it. The sight of the carriage gave his stomach a turn. It was the prison carriage, and if they were placing him in the prison carriage then that must mean that Dafydd had something up his sleeve that included having Owain out of the way. He clenched his teeth in frustration. Why hadn't he done something more about this? How could he have let Dafydd take the crown and not done something more to prevent him from becoming a ruler in place of his father?

Royal slid open the carriage door, and they pushed Owain inside, sliding it shut behind him with a bang. The interior of the carriage smelled stale, and the floor felt spongy with some sort of straw-like material. There were no benches or anything in here, and so he sat down in the corner and leaned his back against the wall and crossed his legs. A few minutes later, he felt the carriage begin to move and heard the clopping of the horse's hooves on stone, and the creaking of the castle gate as it opened. Then he heard it clang shut behind and felt the carriage slowly start to pick up speed as they drove down the road into the town.

It didn't take very long to reach the town jail. The carriage stopped and the door was opened by Jefferies, letting sunlight flood into the dark interior. Owain was led out of the carriage and a short distance to the front doors of the jailhouse. This seemed to be a large house with about four or five rooms with doors that were locked. A large thick-bodied man of medium height, with short graying hair and round amber eyes, answered the door when Royal knocked.

"Yes," He said in a gruff voice, looking at the two guards standing there holding on to Owain.

"We have a prisoner who has been sent to stay here by the Prince until he can be transferred on," Royal explained. The man said nothing and simply nodded his head and beckoned them inside.

"You can put him in the first room on the right at the end of the hall," the man said, pointing to a hall that led away to the right of the door. Straight ahead was a set of stairs that Owain assumed went up to rooms above where the jail keeper and his family must live. Royal nodded his head in thanks, and they marched Owain off in the direction the man had indicated.

The room they put him in was small with a single-high window which was barred. The room consisted of a single bed frame, a chamber pot, and a small table that sat beside the bed.

The room smelled dank, and the floor was coated with dirt as if the place had never been cleaned. The mattress on the bed was stuffed with wool and had a large stain in the middle of it. A thick ragged blanket lay folded next to the single flat pillow. Everything about the room made Owain's skin crawl. He didn't even want to think about how many bugs there must be in the place. Jefferies undid the cuffs from his wrists, and he rubbed at them in relief.

"You will wait here until someone comes to collect you," Jefferies said.

"Collect me for what exactly? What is going on?" Owain demanded.

"Believe us, we know no more than you do," Royal said.

"Sure," Owain said sarcastically.

Royal shrugged and left the room followed closely by his brother.

Owain sank down onto the bed as the door shut with a bang and he heard the key scrape in the lock. Maybe they were telling the truth and they didn't know any more about this than he did. He wished he knew what his uncle was up to. He lay down on the bed and tried to clear his mind of thought. Whatever would come, he knew he had no control over any of it. As he lay on the bed with his eyes closed he began to realize that what he was feeling was not anger but fear. He didn't know what was going to happen to him, and for the first time in his life, he was truly afraid. He wished his father was back from his mission. He would know what to do. He always knew what to do. He curled himself into a ball and tried to slow the beating of his heart and tried again to clear his mind of all thought. Then, ever so slowly, he began to breathe deeper and deeper, and after a few minutes, he had fallen fast asleep fully clothed and with a mind consumed with worry about his fate.

Chapter 6

The Tower of London

Aberfraw Castle, Clwyd Valley, Gwynedd, Wales

Two weeks later…

It was a beautiful sunny afternoon when Gruffudd returned home from a scouting mission to the southern border. It was a part of his duties as the head warrior to travel to the different borders and collect what information he could about the state of things. Along the way, he would stop in to visit with some of the lesser nobles under his brother's rule and find out if there was anything they needed, or sometimes just get the local gossip of the land. He was generally well-liked among the nobles of Gwynedd, and so they would most often talk quite openly with him about all kinds of matters. He had even from time to time been invited to stay with some of the rulers in the lands to the south. But that was not very often. He always made sure to do the best he could to keep the relationship between his family, and the rest of the nobles of Gwynedd and as many of the royals to the south in harmony, and he had managed the feat now for over twenty years. He had become the unofficial ambassador for his family when his father was still ruler of Gwynedd and had simply continued in this role after his father had died and his brother had become ruler in his place.

As he rode up to the castle gates, the guard on duty waved at him in greeting. He smiled and waved back. The guard opened the gate for him, and with a nod of thanks, he rode through into the courtyard beyond. He stopped in the middle of the courtyard and dismounted. A young groom from the stables took the reins of his horse to take her to the stables. Rummaging in his pocket, he found a coin and pulling it out placed it in the boy's hand.

"Thank you," the boy said and pocketed the coin. Gruffudd smiled at him and turning away walked up to the front doors of the castle.

He saw the guard Cammo standing there in front of the castle doors with a welcoming smile on his face and smiled at him in return. He had always liked Cammo. He had even fought with the man in battle before he had injured himself and retired from soldiering to take on guard duty at the castle instead. A much safer if not quite as exciting a job.

"Cammo, it is good to see you, old friend," he said as he walked up to the man. Cammo smiled and bowed his head to him.

"It is good to see you as well, My Lord," Cammo said a little awkwardly. He had always had a hard time knowing how to respond when Gruffudd greeted him so. "How was your trip?"

"It was pleasant," Gruffudd said with another small smile. "The nobles I stayed with were all very happy to see me and pleased to know that Gwynedd still has a ruler. I think they were worried that after my father died we would all be at the mercy of the English, but thankfully their worries were unnecessary in the end."

"Yes, it is good to know that we are safe from the English again as long as the Prince is up to the job," Cammo agreed. Gruffudd shook his head. He still couldn't think of his brother as a Prince even though he had been there and witnessed his coronation. It was hard to believe it had been just a little over three months since it had happened. Time flies when you are having fun he thought.

"How are things going around here?" he asked. Cammo shrugged uncomfortably.

"Well, all right I suppose given what has happened to Lord Owain," he said avoiding Gruffudd's gaze.

"What are you talking about? What has happened to my son?" Gruffudd demanded. Cammo groaned inwardly. He had known Gruffudd for many years and felt very sorry about the fate of his eldest son.

"Lord Owain was arrested and taken to the town jail," he explained.

"On what charges?" Gruffudd asked.

"Don't know," Cammo said honestly. "All I know is I saw him marched out of the castle in cuffs by the two guards, Royal and Jefferies and put into the prison carriage, which was then driven out of the castle gates and down the road to the town. I heard later from Royal that he had been placed in the town jailhouse."

Gruffudd took a few deep breaths to keep his voice steady. "When?"

"About two weeks ago My Lord," Cammo replied.

"Thank you for telling me," Gruffudd said.

"I am just sorry I don't have any more information for you. Perhaps you should ask the Prince," Cammo suggested.

"I will do so," Gruffudd said. Cammo opened the front doors then, and Gruffudd walked through into the front hall.

He started walking off in the direction of his room. There was no way he was going to go and talk to his brother without first seeing his wife Sanena. She was his world and he hers. He had been gone for nearly six weeks now and he ached to hold her in his arms again. Her faith in him was sometimes the only thing that kept him going when for one reason or another he felt like he could no longer continue they had made a pact to one another that they would never give up on each other, and they never had. Her love was a balm to him, and he always took her with him in his heart when he went away. He had made her a promise that he would never leave her alone, and he had done his best to keep that promise. They had four beautiful children that kept her company when he had to go away, and he always felt comforted by the knowledge.

When he reached his room he knocked once and opened the door. Sanena was sitting by the fire embroidering a piece of cloth that lay upon her lap and looked up when the door opened. Seeing her husband standing there in the doorway, she stood up dropping the cloth and rushed over to embrace him. He met her halfway across the room and pulling her into his arms kissed her. "Lord, how I have missed you," he said as they broke from the kiss.

"I can tell," she said with a smile. "I have missed you too."

"Yeah, how much?"

"More than you could ever imagine," she said with a big smile on her lips.

"Come here you," he said and picking her up in his arms carried her laughing to the bed.

A little while later they lay together on their bed trying to remember how to breathe. Sanena turned her head to look at her husband lying there beside her in total abandon. She drew her gaze down the length of his body, taking in every inch of him as if there was nothing more important in the world than to imprint the image of him in her mind. Every scar on his well-muscled body told a story of some battle he had fought in at one time or another as a warrior in the royal army. She had nursed him through many of his wounds over the years, and so knew some of the scars intimately. To some, the scars would have been seen as flaws, but to her, it made him even more beautiful than if his body had been completely unmarked. They were just another part of him, and she loved every part of him.

He saw her looking at him and smiled. "Like what you see?" he asked. The light from the fire played over her face and body making them glow with light. At that moment, he didn't think he had ever seen anything else quite as beautiful as his wife's naked body glowing with firelight.

She smiled back at him. "Oh, yes," she said.

He laughed and pulled her into his arms. She rested her head against his shoulder and closed her eyes.

"I love you," he said. She opened her eyes and looked up at him.

"I love you too," she said. He took a deep breath in and let it out once more.

"I heard about Owain," he said.

"Oh," she said. She had wanted to be the one to tell him of their son's unfortunate fate, but it looked like someone had beat her to it. "Who told you?"

"Cammo told me," he said.

"Oh," she said again. She should have guessed. They had been friends of a sort for many years now and had fought together on the battlefield which could form a kind of bond of its own.

"Has Owain done anything wrong?" he asked.

"Not that I am aware of," she said. "He has mostly been keeping his head down and trying to stay out of Dafydd's way."

"I wonder what is going on then?" he said.

"I don't know," she said. "He was asking me about Llywelyn not that long ago as well."

"What about him?"

"He wanted to know if I had any information on where he is. I told him I didn't have a clue," she said.

"Is he not back yet?" he asked.

"No," she replied.

"I wonder what is keeping him?" he said.

"Oh, you know Llywelyn. He often goes off by himself for weeks at a time without telling anyone where he is going or how long he will be gone. At least he has Olan with him," she said.

"True enough," he said and giving her a final squeeze rolled away from her and sat up.

"I think I need to go and see my brother and find out what is going on," he said standing up and beginning to dress.

"Yes, I think that is a good idea," she said continuing to lie on the bed while she watched him dress. He finished dressing and sat down on the bed to lace his boots. Then he leaned down and kissed Sanena softly on the lips before standing up once more and walking to the bedroom door. At the door, he stopped and turned back to face her. She smiled at him and blew a kiss in his direction. He smiled back.

"I love you," he said once more.

"I love you too," she said. He stood there looking at her for another few seconds all the while wishing he had hours, or even better days to just stand there and look at his wife. He finally managed to pull his eyes from his wife and opening the door left the room. Gruffudd walked through the halls to his brother's room thinking about his second eldest son Llywelyn. He wondered where he was. He hoped that the lad hadn't gotten himself in trouble somehow. The last thing they needed was for Llywelyn to end up in prison as well. He wondered what Owain could have possibly done to merit him taking some jail time. He hoped his temper hadn't gotten a hold of him or something like that. Owain's hot head had gotten him in trouble quite a lot over the years. He just couldn't control himself as well as Llywelyn could.

He reached his brother's room and knocked.

"Come in," Dafydd called from inside. Gruffudd opened the door and went inside. Dafydd was sitting by the fire reading a book as he entered. He looked up when Gruffudd entered the room, and seeing who it was he closed the book and put it down beside his chair.

"Gruffudd, it is good to see you," he said. "Please, sit down." Gruffudd sat down in the second chair by the fire and began to take a look around at the many tapestries that lined the walls of the room. There seemed to be a couple of new ones that he hadn't seen before. There was one new one in particular that caught his eye. Just the sight of it made him feel a little uneasy. He didn't know why exactly, but that particular tapestry had always made him feel that way. He hadn't seen it in a very long time and wondered where Dafydd had found it.

The picture was of a river at the edge of thick woods. On the bank of the river a stag with a large rack stood taking a drink from the river. In the woods behind the stag out of sight, crouched a hunter with a bow, and he had an arrow trained on the stag ready to be let loose. The last time he had seen the picture it had hung in his father's room. But that had been years ago. He thought it had been lost or maybe thrown away. His mother hadn't liked it much either, but it had been a wedding gift from Gruffudd's grandfather when his parents had married and so his father had felt that he should hang it on the wall to show his thanks. Clearly, he hadn't felt anything when he had looked at it. His mother had gotten her way about it eventually though because it had disappeared after a few years.

"Where did you get that?" he asked pointing at the tapestry.

"Which one are you talking about?" Dafydd asked.

"The one that is hanging above the fireplace," Gruffudd said pointing.

"Oh, that one. I found it among father's things after he died," Dafydd explained.

"I thought father got rid of it years ago because mother hated it so much," Gruffudd said.

"So did I," Dafydd admitted. "But when I was going through his things I found it and decided to hang it here as a reminder of him."

"You know I understood mother's feelings about the thing. It always made me feel a little uneasy whenever I saw it," Gruffudd said with a small shudder.

"I know what you mean," Dafydd said.

"Well, it is your room," Gruffudd said with a shrug.

"How was the mission?" Dafydd asked changing the subject.

"It went well," Gruffudd said. "The southern border is secure, and all of the nobles I stayed with along the way were very courteous to me."

"Did they have any messages or anything?" Dafydd asked.

"Yes. I have them all here with me." Gruffudd said pulling a number of sealed scrolls of parchment out of his pocket and handing them to Dafydd. "There you go."

"Thank you. I will look at these later," Dafydd said, and picking up his book he slid the scrolls inside it for safekeeping and then put it back down again.

"I heard about Owain," Gruffudd said looking into his brother's eyes as he said it. Dafydd blinked once.

"Who told you," he asked suspiciously.

"The guard Cammo," Gruffudd said. "We go way back.

"I see," Dafydd said.

"So, why did you do it then?" Gruffudd asked.

"I arrested him for treason," Dafydd said.

"That is a lie," Gruffudd said in a low menacing voice. "Now why did you really do it?"

"I have my reasons," Dafydd said defiantly.

"Admit it, he got under your skin," Gruffudd said.

"Do you know where your son, Llywelyn is right now?" Dafydd asked.

"No, I do not, and don't change the subject," Gruffudd said.

"Owain was starting to ask too many questions and I could not allow him to continue to undermine my authority," Dafydd said with a shrug.

"Your authority," Gruffudd said with a small smile. Dafydd could practically hear the suppressed laughter in his voice.

"Yes, my authority," he said.

"Whatever you say," Gruffudd said. Dafydd glared at him. He could tell that his brother was making fun of him. "I want to see my son, Dafydd," Gruffudd demanded.

"Oh, don't worry you will be seeing him very soon," Dafydd said.

"Oh, good," Gruffudd said settling himself more comfortably in his chair. He opened his mouth to say something else when there came a knock on the door.

"Come in," Dafydd called. The door opened, and the two guards, Jefferies and Royal walked into the room.

"What is going on?" Gruffudd asked suspiciously.

"I am so sorry, Gruffudd," Dafydd said.

"Sorry about what?" Gruffudd asked.

"These guards are here to arrest you and transport both you and Owain to England where you will be imprisoned in The Tower of London," Dafydd said looking away from his brother's penetrating gaze.

"Are you out of your mind?" Gruffudd demanded. Dafydd looked back at his brother then so that he could see the pain this was going to cause him.

"I had no choice," he said miserably. "A messenger from the King of England came to me a few weeks back with a treaty for me to sign. He is allowing me to keep my land and my title in exchange for both you and Owain."

Gruffudd glared at him. "And so you are going to sell off your own family just like that?" he said disgustedly.

"I had no choice. I couldn't just let the King take all of this after how long and hard our father and grandfather have worked to keep the land free and our people safe," Dafydd exclaimed.

"You always have a choice," Gruffudd said sadly.

"What would you have done then in my place?" Dafydd demanded.

"I would have fought harder to find a way to get what I wanted without having to sacrifice my own family," Gruffudd said harshly.

"You are a fool," Dafydd said.

"No, Dafydd, you are the fool if you think for one second the King will keep his word. He has no reason to do so, and mark my words he will do anything he can to get his hands on Gwynedd. You just watch," Gruffudd said.

"I know you don't believe me, but I am sorry about this," Gruffudd shook his head and stood up.

"I am ready," he said to the guards. They stood on either side of him, and both took one of his arms and marched him out of the room. Dafydd watched him as they left hoping his brother would look at him just one more time, but he never did. Feeling like he had a block of ice in his stomach he stood up and left the room to follow them.

He was almost at the front doors when he heard the sound of running footsteps. He stopped in his tracks and turning saw that it was Sanena running towards him. She skidded to a halt in front of him gasping for breath.

"Dafydd, what is going on?" she croaked Dafydd said nothing and walked up to the front doors which were opened for him by another guard and walked through into the courtyard beyond followed closely by Sanena.

The moment they stepped outside, he regretted not grabbing his cloak, for rain was pelting down out of the sky and they were both soaked through in seconds. As they walked into the courtyard they saw Gruffudd being put into the same prison carriage that had transported Owain to the town jailhouse about two weeks previously. With a cry of despair, Sanena ran forward just as the door was being slid closed behind her husband. Hearing her cry, he put a hand on the door to keep it from closing completely and gave her a look of such deep love that it made Dafydd feel such deep anguish for the two of them.

Looking over he saw the tears coursing down Sanena's face as she stared back at Gruffudd just as intently. Then Gruffudd took his hand off the door, and Royal slid it closed with a bang and they could see him no more.

As the carriage began to roll towards the front gate she turned around and lifting her hand she slapped Dafydd hard across the face. He flinched as his head was thrown back with the strength of the blow, and felt a trickle of blood run down his chin from where her wedding band had cut his lip.

"You did this!" she cried and raised her hand to strike him a second time. He took a hold of her wrists, and holding her at a distance looked into her eyes as he spoke. He saw how wild her eyes had become, and was glad he had thought to take hold of both of her wrists instead of just one; otherwise, she looked like she would have tried to scratch his eyes out if she had the chance.

"Calm down," he said in a calm and measured tone. She was practically foaming at the mouth now.

"You are right, it is my fault," he said trying to show her with his eyes how truly sorry he was. "But I had no choice." She took several deep breaths and tried to regain some self-control. He smiled at her and gave her wrists a light squeeze. "Come on, let's get inside before we are drowned." He let go of her and started walking back towards the castle. She followed him in silence, and they walked back through the front doors and into the front hall. The servant Huw saw them and came running up to them.

"My Prince is everything all right?" he asked.

"Everything is fine Huw. Can you bring a large decanter of brandy to my room and a couple of Elsa's meat pies if she has any? I am suddenly feeling rather hungry," Dafydd said. Huw nodded his head.

"Yes, of course, My Prince," he said and ran off to do his Prince's bidding. Dafydd walked back to his room and Sanena followed still not talking. When they reached his room he pulled two chairs as close to the fire as was possible without actually sitting in it and sitting down in one he pointed to the second. Seeing this Sanena walked over to the chair and sat down facing him. They sat in silence for a minute or so trying to warm up from their trip out into the rain. Huw entered the room carrying a decanter of brandy, as well as two cups and a meat pie with its pastry greasy and flaky. He placed it all on the small table in the corner of the room and giving a small bow left once more, shutting the door behind him as he left. Dafydd stood up and walked over to the table. He poured brandy into the two cups and carrying both cups in one hand and the meat pie in the other walked back to the fire. He placed one of the cups in Sanena's hand and sitting down again took a bite of the pie. She nodded her head in thanks and took a sip of her brandy. After she had taken a few heartening sips she cleared her throat and looked at her brother-in-law.

"Does this have anything to do with that messenger that came here from England two weeks ago?" she asked taking another sip of brandy. He finished chewing his bite of pie and smiled at her powers of deduction.

"Yes," he replied. "He came here with a peace treaty from the King for me to sign saying that if I sent him

Gruffudd and Owain that he would allow me to keep my lands and title."

"And if you disagreed, he would start a war between our two lands and take everything your father and your grandfather before him has fought so hard for," she said taking another sip of brandy.

"Exactly," he said. "So you can understand what kind of a bind this puts me in. Believe me, I never wanted to do this, and that it cuts deeper than you could ever know."

"What do we do now? Without my husband, as head warrior, we are left quite vulnerable," she observed.

"All we can do now is wait for your son, Llywelyn to return. It is all on him now," Dafydd said taking another bite of pie.

"Yes, he is his father's son. He will make a fine job of it," she said.

He broke off a piece of pie and handed it to her. She took it with a nod of thanks and bit into it hungrily. Chewing industriously she washed it down with more brandy from her cup.

A short time later the carriage stopped at the town jailhouse and the guard Royal went inside to collect Owain. Gruffudd lay in the corner of the carriage wondering what his life would be like from now on when the door was slid open, and his son Owain was shoved inside with him. Owain cursed as the door was shut behind him and he fell heavily on his side on the spongy reeking straw that covered the floor of the carriage.

"Hello, son," Gruffudd said.

Owain swore again. "So, they got you to then did they?" he said.

"Yes," Gruffudd said sitting up.

"Do you have any idea where they are taking us?" Owain asked sitting up and placing his back against the door.

"Apparently, we are to be taken to The Tower of London in England," Gruffudd said placing his back against the wall and stretching his legs out in front of him.

"I don't understand. Why is he doing this?" Owain said confused.

"He was forced into a treaty with the King and we were the price to keep him from taking over Gwynedd," Gruffudd explained.

"Or so he says," Owain said scathingly. "Maybe he just wanted us out of the way so he could do whatever he wanted without having to be accountable for his actions."

"I don't think so," Gruffudd said with a yawn. "Not this time." He lay down then, and closing his eyes fell asleep, leaving Owain alone in the dark with his thoughts as they rolled ever onwards towards England and The Tower of London.

Chapter 7

An Unexpected Homecoming

Meanwhile, farther away in the Welsh countryside, Llywelyn came awake one morning drenched in a cold sweat. He didn't understand why, but he felt like there was something terribly wrong. The smell of pine was strong under the trees that Llywelyn and Olan had camped under to keep themselves safe from the pounding rain. Even with the tree's protection, his blanket was still stiff with damp when he woke. But it was nothing that he hadn't dealt with before. Cold and wet were just a part of life when you were a warrior like himself who traveled the countryside on a regular basis.

He sat up and looked around the clearing. They hadn't bothered with a fire the night before because they couldn't find any wood that wasn't waterlogged. The early morning light was dimmed by the tree branches, but there was just enough light to see their horses standing under another tree on the opposite side of the clearing, but nothing beyond. They didn't seem distressed by anything though. Turning his head he saw that Olan was still fast asleep on his back a short distance from him. Olan was almost as light a sleeper as himself, so if there had truly been something wrong he would have woken up as well. Breathing a little better, he stood up and walked over to where they had placed their saddlebags and picked up the water skins that lay beside them, and turning walked off into the trees to find water.

He fought his way through the wet undergrowth trying to understand why he felt so strongly that there was something wrong. He tried to remember his dreams, but they eluded him. He rarely remembered his dreams, and so wasn't surprised he couldn't recall them now.

He finally broke through the trees onto the bank of a small stream, and kneeling down began to fill the water skins. He tried to lose himself in the soothing sound of the water running over the rocks and clear his mind, but no matter how hard he tried he still couldn't shake his unsettled feeling. After he finished filling the skins, he splashed the cold water on his face and cupping his hands scooped up handfuls of water to drink. Once he had drunk his fill he stood up, and carrying the skins carefully so they wouldn't spill, he began to fight his way through the undergrowth once more.

When Llywelyn returned to the clearing he saw that Olan was awake, and looking through the saddlebags for something cold to eat for breakfast. He looked up when he heard Llywelyn's footsteps.

"Good morning," Llywelyn said laying the water skins carefully on the ground.

"There you are," Olan said sounding relieved. "Are you all right?"

"Yes, I am fine," Llywelyn said with a smile. "I just went to get some water. Is there anything to eat?"

"Not much. I wish we could make a fire then at least we could have some tea," Olan said pulling out what was left of their dried meat supply and dividing it into two portions he handed one to Llywelyn. He took it with a nod of thanks and put a piece in his mouth, chewing industriously. Dried meat was not the best thing for breakfast, but it was all they had.

"Maybe we will get lucky this evening and find some dry wood. There has to be some around. Maybe deeper into the trees where the rain doesn't penetrate as much," Llywelyn said, putting the second piece of meat into his mouth and chewing.

"Let's hope so," Olan said beginning to eat his own portion of the dried meat. He couldn't even remember what kind it was. Once it was dried out all meat tasted the same to him.

Llywelyn sat down and pulling a water skin towards him washed down the meat with water. That was the one thing about cured meat; it tended to dry out one's mouth.

"How far do you think we are from Aberfraw Castle?" Llywelyn asked after a time.

"About a week I think," Olan said. "Why?"

"I woke up this morning with a feeling like something terrible has happened. But I don't know why."

"Did you have a bad dream or something?" Olan asked.

"No, I don't think so," Llywelyn said. "Not that I remember them anyway."

"Well, we should be home shortly in any case," Olan said trying to sound cheerful. He wanted to get back home as well and see that young woman Talia again. He had not stopped thinking about her the entire time they had been away. He had barely talked to her, but she had left a lasting impression on him and he couldn't get her out of his mind.

Olan took the second water skin and gave the horses some water while Llywelyn packed the blankets back into the saddlebags. Then between the two of them, they managed to saddle both of the horses and buckle on the saddlebags in record time. They mounted up and rode out of the clearing and started on the road back to Aberfraw Castle.

They returned home about a week later to find that things had changed since they had been away. The people in the town and the village seemed unsettled and stared at Llywelyn as he passed in a very unsettling way.

"Something is wrong," Olan said seeing the way that the people were looking at them as they rode through the village and town on the way to the castle.

"I know," Llywelyn said. It had been about three weeks since Gruffudd and Owain had been taken to England, and it was still the main topic of conversation in the town and the village. Gruffudd had been widely respected and his loss, coupled with the loss of Owain, had affected the people very deeply.

As they rode towards the castle, Llywelyn longed for a hot bath and a good night's sleep in a real bed. They reached the castle gates, and the guard on the gates gave Llywelyn a quick nod of greeting which he returned.

"It is good to see you home again, Lord Llywelyn," the guard said.

"It is good to be home," Llywelyn said with a smile. The guard opened the gate and they rode through into the courtyard. They dismounted and Olan took the horses off in the direction of the stables. Llywelyn walked up to the front doors and found the guard Cammo standing in front of them. He gave the man a quick smile and Cammo gave him a respectful nod in return.

"Hello Cammo, how are you?" he asked. Cammo smiled at him. He had grown to be such a nice young man. He reminded Cammo vividly of his father when he had been young. Not just in looks but also in the way he treated everyone around him with respect no matter who they were.

"I am fine thank you, Lord Llywelyn. How was your trip?" he asked.

"It was good thanks," Llywelyn said. "How are things around here? How is my mother?" Cammo sighed.

"She is all right I suppose given the circumstances," he said.

"What are you talking about?" Llywelyn asked apprehensively. "What has happened since I have been away?"

"Your father and brother Owain were taken to England about three weeks ago to be imprisoned there in The Tower of London," Cammo said.

"What?" Llywelyn asked outraged. He didn't understand how this could have happened.

"How did this happen?" he asked.

"I don't know, My Lord. Perhaps you should ask the Prince yourself," Cammo suggested.

"Oh, don't worry, I will," Llywelyn said. "Thank you for telling me about my father and my brother."

"I thought you should know," Cammo said.

"Well, thanks again," Llywelyn said with a small smile of appreciation. Cammo opened the castle doors then, and Llywelyn walked through into the front hall.

The servant Huw saw Llywelyn and gave him a small bow.

"My Lord, it is good to see you home," he said.

"Thank you Huw, it is good to be home," Llywelyn said. "Do you know where my uncle is Huw?" Huw nodded his head.

"Yes, My Lord. He is in the great hall finishing a late lunch," Huw said.

"Thank you Huw," Llywelyn said and turning headed off in the direction of the great hall.

His heart was pounding in his chest with uncontrollable rage. He just couldn't understand why Dafydd would have done such a thing. It didn't make any sense. How could he just send his own brother and nephew off like that? Then another thought entered his mind. Was Dafydd going to send him off to England to join his father and brother as well? He would like to see him try he thought as he reached the great hall. He pushed open the door and went inside without knocking.

He marched up to the head table where Dafydd sat reading some papers and stopped. Dafydd looked up from his papers and gave a little jump of surprise to see Llywelyn standing there.

"Llywelyn, I didn't hear you come in. It is good to see you. How are you?" he asked sitting a little straighter in his chair.

"What have you done?" Llywelyn demanded.

"I don't know what you are talking about," Dafydd said picking up his cup and taking a sip of brandy.

"Don't try to play coy with me," Llywelyn snarled. "Why did you send my father and my brother to England to be imprisoned in The Tower of London?"

Dafydd sighed. "Sit down and have a cup of brandy. You look like you could use one," he said.

Llywelyn walked around to the other side of the table and sat down facing his uncle across the table.

Dafydd poured brandy into a cup and handed it to his nephew. Llywelyn took it, and lifting it to his mouth took a long swallow before placing it back on the table and focusing his gaze on Dafydd's face once more.

"So?" he said waiting to hear an explanation.

"Who told you?" Dafydd asked.

"Does it really matter?" Llywelyn said.

"No, I suppose not," Dafydd said draining the last few drops from his cup and then refilling it.

"A messenger from the King of England came to me several weeks ago with a treaty for me to sign saying that I can keep my land in exchange for Gruffudd and Owain," Dafydd explained taking another drink of brandy.

Llywelyn shook his head. "Do you truly believe the King will leave it at that?" he asked taking a sip from his own cup.

"I have no choice but to believe he will keep his word. We do have a signed agreement and that should count for something," Dafydd said taking another sip.

"I don't know," Llywelyn said skeptically. "He is the King of England. Who knows what he is capable of?"

Dafydd shrugged and took yet another sip of brandy from his cup.

"So what happens now?"

"Well, with your father gone we need another head warrior to patrol the borders and liaison with the nobles of Gwynedd and such," Dafydd said.

"I agree," Llywelyn said.

"I would like you to do it," Dafydd said.

"Me?" Llywelyn said surprised.

"Yes. You are the best warrior in the land next to your father and I truly don't know anyone else that is good enough for the job. You are good with people, and the people like you and talk to you. You have no idea how valuable such a talent like that can be," Dafydd said.

Llywelyn looked appraisingly at his uncle. He had changed since becoming ruler and he didn't quite know what to make of the man. "All right, I'll do it," he said after a minute or so had passed.

"Thank you," Dafydd said.

"If the land needs me then I will do what I can to help," Llywelyn said draining the last few drops from his cup.

"All right then, come to my room later and we can go over your new responsibilities now that you are head warrior," Dafydd said.

"I look forward to it," Llywelyn said pushing back his chair and standing up. "I need to go and change out of these traveling clothes. Excuse me," he said and with a nod to his uncle left the hall once more.

He entered his room a few minutes later to find that Olan had returned from tending to the horses. Seeing Llywelyn, Olan stood up from the hearth where he had been stoking the fire he had built a short time before.

"How was the Prince?" he asked brushing soot off his hands.

"Not bad," Llywelyn said sitting down on the bed and sighing with pleasure to be sitting on something soft after riding on horseback for days. "He told me the whole story."

"And?" Olan prompted.

"It was either sign a treaty with the King of England and send him my father and brother or lose everything," Llywelyn said stretching his shoulders to try and loosen the knots he could feel there.

"I see," Olan said sitting down at the table and turning to face him. "Did he say anything else?"

"Yes," Llywelyn said beginning to stretch his back as best he could. "He wants me to become the head warrior in my father's place."

"Really?" Olan said intrigued. The position of the head warrior was quite an honor. But if there was anyone fit for the job it was Llywelyn, no question.

"Yes," Llywelyn said.

"Did you accept?" Olan asked.

"Yes, I did. I have to go to his room later to find out what my new responsibilities will be," Llywelyn said with a hint of excitement in his voice. He was sad about his father and his brother, but the chance to be the head warrior at such a young age was nothing to be scoffed at. He recognized that this was the opportunity of a lifetime, and he would do his best to see it through.

"Well, I am happy for you," Olan said. "About the new job I mean. It is terrible what has happened to your father and brother, but it sounds like there wasn't much choice about it. After all, Dafydd couldn't very well let Gwynedd fall into the hands of the English after all your grandfather and his father before him have done to keep the land and the people free," Llywelyn nodded his head in agreement.

"I think I will go and see my mother and see how she is doing. Right after I get changed. I smell like a horse," Llywelyn said standing up and walking over to his closet. He quickly changed into fresh clothes and after running a comb through his hair he turned towards the door. "I will see you later," he said pulling open the door.

"Say hello for me," Olan said.

"Will do," Llywelyn said and left the room.

Llywelyn reached his mother's room and knocked.

"Come in," she called from inside. He opened the door then and walked into the room. He saw his mother sitting by the fire and having her hair brushed by the young maid, Talia who stood behind her chair. He could see right away that she was very pretty; especially with the way the firelight seemed to make her hair glow softly. She wasn't his type, but he thought that Olan would probably like her a lot. Little did he know that this was the woman who occupied Olan's every waking thought and haunted his dreams when he slept.

"Hello mother," he said walking a little farther into the room. Sanena smiled with pleasure at seeing her son again after so long.

"Llywelyn, it is so good to see you," she said relieved that he was home once more. "How are you?" He smiled at her.

"I am fine mother," he said. "I heard about father and Owain. I am so sorry. How are you doing?"

"I've been better I won't deny it," she said. "So have you talked to Dafydd then?"

"Yes, and he told me the whole story," Llywelyn said. Sanena reached her hand around and touched Talia's hand to still it.

"That will do for now," she said. "Can you go and fetch some brandy and perhaps a sweet roll if Elsa has one to spare?" Talia nodded. "Yes, of course, right away mam," Talia said, and after placing the brush on the bedside table turned and left the room.

"Nice girl," Llywelyn commented. "Is she new?"

"Yes, she is," Sanena said. "Why don't you take a seat." She pointed to the other chair that sat next to the fire, and nodding he walked over to the chair and sat down facing her.

"I have something I need to tell you," Llywelyn said settling himself more comfortably in his chair.

"Oh?" Sanena prompted.

"Dafydd asked me if I would take on the job of the head warrior and I accepted. I have to go to his room later to find out what my new responsibilities will be in the new position," he said. She smiled at him. She knew he would take the job. He was great with people and was no stranger to traveling and sleeping rough when he had to.

"I am so proud of you," she said beaming. "This is such a great opportunity for you. Congratulations."

He grinned back at her. "I am so happy you agree. It could be dangerous, and things could go wrong," he said.

"All such things come with danger, but your father came to no harm so I am sure you will be just fine too," she said.

Talia was walking back from the kitchen carrying a stone bottle of brandy in one hand and a sweet roll in the other. When turning a corner, she almost collided with Olan coming in the opposite direction.

"Oh, I'm so sorry," he said.

"It is fine really," she said. "You work for Lord Llywelyn, right?"

"Yes, I do. I'm Olan," he said feeling flustered. She was standing close enough that he could smell the scent of wood smoke on her wool dress and see the way her chest rose and fell as she breathed.

"I am Talia. It is nice to meet you, Olan," she said.

"Yes," Olan said. His head felt slow and his mouth seemed to have gone very dry all of a sudden.

"Well, I should be going. I have to take this brandy and roll to Lady Sanena," she said giving him a smile. "See you around Olan." She turned then and started off in the direction of Sanena's room once more.

Olan stood staring after her feeling like he had just been punched in the stomach. His legs felt weak, and he couldn't remember how to walk for a second or two as if her smile had paralyzed him somehow and rooted him to the spot. Finally, he shook his head and managed to start putting one foot in front of the other, and in that slow and awkward fashion, he walked back down the hall to Llywelyn's room, forgetting that he had come out to go and get them both dinner so there would be food when he returned from talking with his mother.

Talia knocked once on Sanena's door and entered the room.

"I have your brandy and food, mam," she said and walking over to the bedside table placed brandy, cups, and sweet roll on it.

"Thank you, Talia," Sanena said with a smile.

"Will you be needing anything else, mam?" Talia asked.

"No, thank you. You can go now and take a break for a while," Sanena said.

"Thank you. mam," Talia said and left the room once more. Sanena stood up and walked over to the table. She poured brandy into the two cups and carried both the cups and the sweet roll back over to the fire. She handed one of the cups to her son, and breaking the roll in two, gave him half before biting into the other.

"Thank you," he said biting into his half. He took a long swallow of brandy to wash down the roll.

"Are you nervous?" she asked.

"A little, but I am excited as well," he admitted, taking another swallow of brandy.

"I know you will do well," she said taking a sip from her own cup.

"Thank you," he said draining his cup. "I should go and see him now."

"Of course," she said with an encouraging smile. He smiled back and standing up left the room.

He reached his uncle's room and knocked.

"Come in," Dafydd called from inside. Llywelyn opened the door and stepped into the room, shutting the door behind him.

"Llywelyn, please sit down." Llywelyn walked over to the fire and sat down facing his uncle.

"I have come to find out what you require of me in my new position," he said.

"Yes, of course," Dafydd said with a small smile. "Well like I said before I will need you to liaison with the nobles of Gwynedd, and also I will need you to scout from time to time as well as do border patrol," Dafydd explained.

"Is that everything?" Llywelyn asked.

"For now. When we go to battle I will need you to work with Captain Carrol and lead the army. But that is unlikely for a while now that I have signed this treaty with the King," Dafydd said.

"I understand," Llywelyn said. "When do you need me to start?"

"Before your father was taken away he had been on a scouting mission to the southern border and informed me that it was still quite secure. But it is the northern border between us and England that concerns me more. Even though I have signed this treaty I don't fully trust that he will keep his word. I will need you to gather enough supplies for three weeks and head out in the morning to see the state of the northern border and then come back and report to me once you have done so," Dafydd said.

"Yes, of course. I will leave first thing," Llywelyn said. "Is that everything then?"

"Yes, I think so," Dafydd said.

"Right then," Llywelyn stood up and left the room to find Olan and set him to the task of gathering supplies for another trip into the Welsh countryside.

He returned to his room to find Olan sitting in a chair by the fire and staring blindly into the flames. He looked up at Llywelyn's footsteps and shook himself.

"How did it go with your mother and Dafydd?" he asked.

"Good," Llywelyn said walking over to where he had dropped the saddlebags and sat down to take an inventory of the bags. "Dafydd has set me my first task. I am to leave in the morning for the northern border to ascertain the state of things there and then report back to him."

"How long did he think it would take?" Olan asked.

"He said I would need enough supplies for about three weeks," Llywelyn said.

"I will go and collect the food supplies then. I am sure Elsa has some to spare," Olan said standing up.

"Good," Llywelyn said. Olan left the room then with a sense of excitement. Maybe he would see the young woman Talia again. But he didn't want to get his hopes up. He was very proud of Llywelyn for getting his opportunity, and he promised himself that he would support him in any way he needed to make his job as easy as possible. He could feel that this was a new chapter in their lives, and he was excited. Who knew what the future would bring them now? As awful as it was that Lord Gruffudd had been taken to England, it had opened the door for Llywelyn to make a name for himself. He smiled to himself, and with a spring in his step made his way through the halls to the kitchen.

The next morning Sanena stood in the courtyard watching her son ride away down the road away from the castle on his first mission as head warrior. Despite her worry as his mother, she was filled with pride. This was the opportunity of a lifetime and she was very happy for him. She reminded herself that he had Olan with him, and she knew that he would protect Llywelyn with his life. She waited until they were out of sight and then turned and went back into the castle once more.

Llywelyn spent the next four years fulfilling his duties as head warrior and enjoying himself thoroughly even though he spent a lot of time away from home he had to report back and so was able to keep in touch with his family and keep abreast of how things were at home. Olan would make sure to see the young woman Talia each time they returned to the castle, and over time they started a relationship that they were able to keep going despite the fact that he left all the time. It was the way of life when you were the servant of the head warrior of Gwynedd, but he never complained. He loved his job. He had made a promise that he would never leave his side and he planned to keep that promise no matter what.

Chapter 8

The King's Proposal

The Tower of London, London, England, 1244 AD

About four years later, Owain lay on the stone floor of his tower cell in The Tower of London, when he was brought awake by the sound of footsteps on the landing outside the cell door. He heard the sound of keys in the lock, and the door opened a moment later. A guard entered the room carrying a tray with two bowls of food on it. Light from torches in brackets on the wall outside the cell door cast shadows on the cell walls and momentarily blinded Owain as he sat up. The guard laid the tray on the ground before Owain.

"Food," the man said and backed out of the room. These guards were nothing like the ones he had known back home. They were rougher looking and had absolutely no sense of humor. The guard shut the cell door and locked it once more. Owain waited until the guard's footsteps had disappeared before turning his head to the bundle of rags that lay against the wall on the other side of the cell.

"Food's here." The bundle of rags, which was his father, stared and opened his eyes. The man was emaciated and ghostly pale, and Owain could see every bone in his body.

"You eat it," he mumbled and closed his eyes once more. Owain shrugged his shoulders in frustration.

"That is what you always say," he said, exasperated. Gruffudd opened his eyes and looked at his son.

"What is it to you if I eat or not," he snapped. Owain glared at his father.

"It matters to me because I refuse to watch my father slowly killing himself by starvation," he said his voice full of emotion.

"Leave me alone," Gruffudd growled, and closing his eyes, he turned away from his son. Owain glared at the back of his head and then began to eat. He finished off both bowls and then lay back down on the floor and closed his eyes.

He was brought awake once more a few hours later by a grunting sound. It sounded like some kind of large animal trying to move its ponderous body. It was deep in the night now, so the sky outside the tower window was pitch black. He sat up and rubbed his eyes, trying to clear them. He waited for them to adjust to the darkness before looking around the tower for the source of the sound.

Even after his eyes adjusted to the dark, it was still very hard to see anything. But after a moment, he spotted the source of the strange sound and found that it was his father attempting to climb the tower wall using a rope made from his ragged clothing. He jumped up and ran over to his father with his heart racing with panic. He didn't know what to do. He didn't want to scare him and cause him to fall. But on the other hand, it wasn't like he could just stand there and watch him struggle either.

"What are you doing?" he cried in fright. Blood streaked the wall from several scratches on Gruffudd's hands, feet, and knees as he continued to clamber laboriously up the tower wall towards the window at the very top of the wall. Owain didn't know how he was managing to do it. Not with the condition he was in. It must have been pure stubbornness that gave him the strength to climb because in every other way he was much too frail.

"What are you doing?" he asked again, still with a note of panic in his voice.

"I am getting out of here," Gruffudd said, growling with effort.

"What are you talking about? Get down from there before you fall and hurt yourself." He was desperate to save his father from the fate he could see unfolding before his eyes, but he was afraid to touch him at the same time.

"I refuse to stay locked up like an animal in a cage any longer," Gruffudd said, grunting with the effort of raising his ruined body ever closer towards the window at the top of the wall. The image was heartbreaking, but Owain didn't look away.

"You are crazy," he said.

"I may seem crazy to you," Gruffudd said, and reaching the window, at last he clung onto the windowsill with both hands. He hung there for a moment to rest and turned his head to look at his son. "Take it from me. Life is not worth living unless you take some risks."

Owain looked up at his father hanging from the windowsill several feet above him and felt his panic expand to new heights.

"I am all for taking a few risks in life," Owain said, trying to keep any sign of fear or panic out of his voice in order not to alarm his father. "Just not stupid ones."

"I am going to get out of here or die trying," Gruffudd said, and using all the strength he had began to pull the rest of his body up to the windowsill. The rough stone scraped his legs where they were exposed, leaving yet more streaks of blood on the wall.

"And how do you plan to get down to the street once you reach the roof?" Owain asked.

"I will figure it out when I get there," Gruffudd said, grunting with effort.

"That sounds great," Owain said with a note of sarcasm in his voice.

"Assuming you don't fall and break your neck getting down to the street. What will you do once you get there? It isn't like you are strong enough to run very far. The guards will recapture you in a second."

"Don't trouble me with details. I will figure these things out when I come to them."

Owain shook his head in exasperation. "Sure you will," he said with a sigh. He could see his father's arms beginning to shake with effort, and as he watched, Gruffudd's hands, slippery with blood, began to slip on the stone of the window ledge.

It almost seemed to happen in slow motion. The makeshift rope snapped, and his hands slipped off the windowsill. Owain reached out his arms to catch his father, but Gruffudd fell through the circle of his arms and landed on the stone floor with the sound of bones snapping.

His chest had suddenly turned into stone, and he couldn't get a breath. Feeling like a drowning man, he knelt to check. But he could see right away that his father had died on impact. His neck was broken, and his head lay at an awkward angle on the floor. He wondered for a moment what else was broken, but didn't check. Tears began to fall unbidden down his face as he looked into his father's star-filled gaze.

"How could you do this to me?" he said as the tears ran faster down his face. "How could you do this to your family? You just couldn't listen to me, could you? No, you always had to do things your way. Well now look where that has gotten you." He threw his head back then and gave one long cry of bone-deep grief and utter despair.

He leapt to his feet and running to the cell door began to pound on it with his fists. "Help! Help!" he called with all the strength he had left in his voice. There came the sound of running footsteps, and a moment later the cell door was flung open. Owain leapt back from the door just in time as a guard came running into the cell.

"What is it? What has happened?" the guard asked. This one was younger with a kind looking face and lake-blue eyes that seemed to smile when he looked at you. Owain looked into the kind face and let the man see his pain.

"My father is dead," he said, his voice breaking on the last word.

"How did this happen?" the guard asked, shocked.

"He was attempting to escape using a makeshift rope and he fell. I think his neck is broken." The guard walked over to where Gruffudd's body lay against the wall and knelt.

"You are right; his neck is broken. I will need to go and fetch someone to help remove the body," the man said standing up. He turned back to Owain and gave him a look of deepest sympathy. Owain gave a small nod of thanks, and the guard left the cell, shutting the door behind him as he left.

Owain sat down beside his father's body to wait and tried to clear his mind and not think about anything in particular. Then about twenty minutes or so later he heard the sound of footsteps in the corridor outside the cell once more. He heard the door being unlocked and then a moment later the guard came back into the room accompanied by a second guard.

This man was a little older than the first. He had short, blond hair streaked with grey and hard black eyes that seemed to say, "I have seen it all." They walked over to where Gruffudd's body lay and picking it up turned to leave the cell. Just before they left the cell the young guard looked into Owain's eyes.

Then he looked away and followed his superior out of the cell, and Owain heard the door slam shut behind them, leaving him alone in the dark empty cell with nothing but his thoughts for company. He curled himself into a ball on the floor and cried as he had never cried in his life. He felt like when his father had died that a part of himself had died with him and that he would never be right again. His world was forever changed now. As he lay there crying, he began to wonder how he was going to tell his family what had happened. His mother and father had been very close, and the news of his death would destroy his mother. He wondered what this would mean for the treaty between the King and his uncle now that his father was dead. Feeling like he had run a mile, he rolled over and closing his eyes fell fast asleep.

About three days later, Owain was brought awake by the sound of footsteps of what sounded like at least three people in the corridor outside his cell. A moment later the door was opened, and three people entered the cell. Owain sat up and saw that two of the people were guards, while the third was someone he had never seen before, but he assumed by the way the man held himself that he must be none other than the King of England himself. He tried not to stare at the man, but it was hard not to. He was nothing like he had expected. He supposed he had been thinking of the man as a hard, gruff, kind of man like the guards he had known for the past four years. But he had a kind face and eyes that seemed to twinkle with suppressed laughter.

The King smiled down at him where he sat on the floor and he suddenly felt very dirty and aware of the fact that he was wearing clothes that were not much better than rags. He thought he must look like a beggar to the King, not Welsh royalty.

"You must be Owain ap Gruffudd."

Owain nodded. "Yes, I am," he said.

"It is a pleasure to meet you at last," Henry said, reaching out his hand. Owain took his hand and shook it briefly, trying not to get too much dirt on the man's well-manicured hand.

"It is an honor to meet you, Your Majesty," he said, his voice rough from disuse. "Forgive me for asking, but what are you doing here?"

"I have come to release you from prison," Henry said with another smile.

"That is very kind of you," Owain said. "Forgive me for asking Your Majesty, but why would you do such a thing for me?"

"Now that your father has died, the treaty between myself and Prince Dafydd is no longer valid," Henry explained. "So I see no reason to keep you here any longer."

Owain couldn't believe what he was hearing. After four long years of imprisonment, the King of England was going to set him free because his father's death had broken the treaty between England and his homeland of Gwynedd, Wales? He didn't know how it could be true, but yet the King was standing in front of him at that very moment and looking down on him with a slight smile on his lips.

Owain cleared his throat. "I don't know what to say," he said truthfully.

Henry smiled at his honesty. "I have also come here today for a different reason," he said.

"Oh?" Owain prompted.

"I have come to make you a proposal," Henry explained.

"I see." Owain felt a little uneasy now. What kind of proposal could a King have for a foreign criminal such as himself? Was this a trap of some kind? He didn't know.

"I want to offer you the chance to change sides and come and join me at my court." Feeling slightly silly sitting there on the floor at the King's feet he stood, and with what dignity he could muster faced the man.

"I am the strategist for the Gwynedd army," he said with pride. "Why on earth would you want me at your court?"

"I could use a good strategist," Henry said with an amused smile. "I want to start a civil war in Gwynedd, and I could use someone who knows the landscape and the nature of the people I would be dealing with."

Owain wanted to laugh. "You want to bring down the Prince?"

"Yes," Henry agreed.

"I am sure he is on borrowed time already. He is only the ruler because he was my grandfather's heir. Not because he is loved by his people," Owain said contemptuously.

"This is what I am talking about," Henry said. "I need such information to have the advantage."

"And what makes you think I would just turn my back on my people so easily?" Owain said, not even bothering to be polite now. He could sense a trap of some kind here and he was determined not to fall into it.

"You would have every luxury at my court and a place in the royal English army."

"There is indeed no love lost between myself and my uncle," Owain admitted. "But that doesn't mean I will just turn my back on my people."

Henry smiled and it made his eyes twinkle. "If you could have anything at all right now, what would that be?" he asked.

Owain looked into the man's eyes and saw the calculation there behind the twinkle.

"A bath," he said honestly.

Laughter rang out in the cell and reverberated off the walls as the King and the guards laughed at his answer.

Then without his bidding, he felt a grin spread across his face and he began to laugh as well for the first time in four years.

"I can get you a bath," Henry said still laughing. "Come and stay at my court as my guest and you can think about my proposal while you recover from your imprisonment. You look like you could use a good long rest and some good food to help build up your strength."

Owain nodded his head in agreement. "You are not wrong there, Your Majesty. Thank you," he said and gave him a small bow from the neck.

"Then let us go. Lead the way," Henry said to the guards and they left the cell and went down the tower stairs to the front doors of the fortress.

As they stepped outside into the sunny afternoon, Owain was momentarily blinded by the light. He hadn't seen the sun for so long now that it was almost too much for his dark-adapted eyes to handle. He looked around the fortress courtyard and saw a large carriage parked a short distance away with two large horses harnessed to the front of it. Owain was a little wary of carriages after being transported to prison in one four years previously. But this one looked much more inviting.

"My carriage is just over here," Henry said leading the way over to it. A footman opened the carriage door and the King slid inside followed by Owain. The door slid shut behind them and a moment later the carriage began to move.

The interior of the carriage was spacious. There were two velvet-covered benches, one on either side of the carriage facing each other. The windows were lined with lace curtains that were held back to let in the light. Owain slid himself along the first bench to the window, and with a small amount of effort managed to slide it open just enough to let in some fresh air. He wanted the feel of the wind on his face.

He sat staring out the window as they rolled through the streets of London. The streets were filled with people, both poor and rich all mixed together. Several people waved at the carriage as it passed through their midst. He thought that the King must be a good ruler to have people waving to him whenever his carriage passed. He doubted his uncle got the same treatment back home.

As they left the city, he began to see fields with sheep and cows and knew they were in the country. As they drove they passed several small villages, and Owain began to relax. This scene was much more like what he remembered back home. He had never been in a big city like London before he had been imprisoned there and the place scared him with its size.

They didn't speak while they drove. Each man sat alone with his thoughts as the carriage rolled ever onward towards Winchester Castle. Owain was so tired he felt like he could sleep for a week. But before he did, he wanted to write his family a letter to tell them what had happened. He wanted them to hear it from him and not to find out about it through the rumor mill.

The carriage arrived at Winchester castle after what felt like several hours later and the carriage was admitted by a courteous nod from the guards as they opened the castle gate. The carriage rolled to a stop in the middle of the courtyard, and the same footman opened the door. The King slid out of the carriage followed by Owain. They walked up to the front door of the castle, which was opened for them by yet another guard.

Once inside, Owain began to look around the place. They stood in the front hall and he saw high ceilings and many different halls leading off of their own. The sheer size of the place overwhelmed Owain. This castle was at least three times as large as Aberfraw.

A servant walked up to them and gave a small bow.

"Your Majesty," the man said.

"Show Lord Owain to a room and find him some fresh clothes and some water to wash with," Henry said. The man nodded his head and turned to Owain.

"Right this way, My Lord." He led him through two hallways before stopping at a door with an ornate brass handle. The servant opened the door and led him inside.

The room was small but comfortable. In one corner there was a small fireplace with a single armchair beside it. The bed sat against the wall across from the door, and in the opposite corner from the fire sat a small table with a chair beside it.

"Here is your room, My Lord," the man said walking over to the fireplace. He knelt and began to build up the fire there. Owain walked over to the bed and sat down gratefully on it. He hadn't sat on something this soft in years and he almost moaned with pleasure. The servant stood up and dusted off his hands as the fire began to crackle merrily.

"I will go and fetch the clothes and water for washing now," he said.

"Thank you," Owain said. Then he remembered that he wanted to write a letter to his family. "Can you also bring some paper and writing implements as well? I want to write a letter to my family."

"Yes, of course, My Lord." He turned then and left the room. He returned a short time later with a kettle full of water in one hand and a basin in the other filled with several items. He walked over to the fire and set the kettle to boil. Then he began to take things out of the basin and lay them on the table. Owain watched as he lay a fresh pile of clothes on the table, as well as soap, washcloth, razor and shaving brush, and all the things needed for writing and sealing a letter. Then he went to check on the water and finding it hot to the touch proceeded to empty the kettle into the basin.

"There you are, My Lord."

"Thank you," Owain said standing up.

"Will you be needing anything else, My Lord?"

"No, thank you." The servant nodded and left the room once more. Owain stripped off the remnants of clothes and began to wash away the dirt and grime of the past four years from his body. When he was finished, he dried off and pulled on the fresh clothes that the King had so generously provided for him—a pair of dark green wool trousers and a matching tunic, as well as thick wool socks and a brand new, pair of tan leather boots.

After he had dawned all of this, he walked over to the mirror and took stock. His face was thin, and he could see large dark circles under his eyes. His hair fell to the middle of his back in waves, and he could see a streak of gray in it. His body was much too thin from not enough food for so long. He felt his stomach gurgle simply with the thought of food and smiled. The smile looked almost strange like he was trying to impose another man's face onto his own. He shook his head and turned away from the mirror.

He walked back to the table and sat down. He pulled a piece of paper towards him and opened the ink well that had been provided. He picked up the quill that lay beside it and dipped it into the ink and he began to write his first letter in four years.

Chapter 9

A Letter from England

Meanwhile, Henry was sitting in his room reading over some army dispatches when there came a knock on the door.

"Come in," he called continuing to read. The door opened, and Lord William entered the room. He looked up and saw his friend standing there in the doorway.

"Ah, Lord William, please sit down." He put the dispatches back on the table and sat up straighter in his chair.

Lord William walked over to the table and sat down opposite the King. "I hear that you have released Lord Owain from prison," he said. It was a statement and not a question.

"Yes, I have," Henry said. "I have brought him back to the castle with me as a guest for the time being.

"Do you think that is wise?" Lord William asked nervously. "He is the enemy after all."

Henry smiled at his friend and Lord Regent. William had always been cautious, sometimes overly so. "I have made him an offer to change sides and join our court," he said.

Lord William shook his head. This was a bad idea. "Did he take the offer?" he asked.

"No, he didn't," Henry said. "I told him he could stay here at the castle for the time being and recover while he thinks over my offer."

"I don't like it," Lord William said honestly. "We don't know what he is capable of."

"Well, that is why I have called you here," Henry explained. "I want you to keep an eye on him and see what you can learn about the man."

"I doubt I will learn much," Lord William said skeptically.

Henry smiled at him. "If there is anyone that can get information from the man it is you," he said with a wink. "Just do your best."

Lord William shrugged. "I will try," he said.

"Thank you," Henry said. Lord William stood up to leave. He gave the King a small bow and then left the room. Leaving him alone with his papers once more.

Owain woke the next morning in a state of confusion. His mind was still foggy with sleep and so it took him a moment to remember where he was and how he had come to be there. The fire had gone out in the night and so the room was icy, making the bed a warm haven. He lay there enjoying the warmth and trying to delay the inevitable. As he lay there, he began to think about his situation and how to use it to his advantage. He was in the castle of the King of England as his guest and he intended to use his time in recovery to learn as much as he could.

Finally resigning himself to the cold, he sat up and pulled back the covers. He felt around the bedside table until he located the candlestick. Finding it and the flint, and steel beside it, he struck a spark and lit the wick of the candle. By its light, he managed to locate his clothes that lay beside the bed. He stood up and shivering quickly pulled on his clothes. He was pulling on his boots when there came a knock on the bedroom door.

"Come in," he called. The door opened and the same servant from the day before entered the room. He gave Owain a small bow of the head in greeting.

"My Lord, the King has asked for you to join him for breakfast in the dining hall this morning," he said.

"Very well," Owain said smiling to himself. He should have expected this he thought. "Lead the way."

The servant led Owain down several halls that seemed to twist and turn through the castle. He kept stock of each turn they took in order not to get lost in the future. The castle seemed immense to him and intimidating. He wondered just how many rooms there were in the place.

They reached the dining hall after what felt like several minutes. The servant opened the hall door and led him inside the hall. He immediately felt out of place. Tables lined the hall on either side of the hall, and finely dressed lords and ladies sat at the tables eating and drinking. He felt their eyes on him as he followed the servant up the center of the hall to the largest and grandest of all the tables that sat upon a raised platform at the end of the hall closest to the fireplace. The King sat at the table surrounded by several members of the royal council.

"Your Majesty, I have brought Lord Owain to dine with you this morning," he said giving the King a bow. Henry turned and saw Owain standing awkwardly at the edge of the platform. He smiled encouragingly and beckoned him to sit.

"You look hungry. Please, sit. And join us," he said pointing to the chair to the right of Lord William. Owain nodded his thanks and walking over to the chair sat down in it. He thought he must look very unusual to everyone in the hall. He wondered if any of them had even seen a Welshman before. With the way they were all looking at him, he guessed he was probably the first.

"Wine?" the King offered.

"Yes, please." Henry poured him a cup and passed it to him.

"Thanks," he said and took a mouthful of the sweet wine. Letting it trickle down the back of his throat before taking another sip.

"Well, let me introduce the royal council," Henry said taking a sip of wine from his cup. "On my right here is Sir Stanley, my best knight," he said pointing to him. Sir Stanley gave a small nod. "And on my left here is Lord William, my Lord Regent. "

"It is a pleasure to meet you at last," Lord William said holding out his hand to Owain. He took it, and they shook hands briefly and then let go.

"Across the table here is Lord Rosen, the Royal Treasurer, and Lord Edmond, my top general," Henry finished explaining.

"It is a pleasure to meet you all," Owain said looking at each man in turn.

"Would you like some sausages, Lord Owain?" Lord Rosen asked.

"Yes, thank you."

Lord Rosen placed a few sausages on a plate along with some fruit and a piece of bread and then handed the plate to Owain. "Here you are My Lord," he said.

"Thank you." Owain picked up a sausage from the plate and bit into it gratefully. It had been a very long time since he had eaten anything like a sausage and this one was better than anything he could have expected. He was so hungry that he could barely keep himself from just swallowing it whole.

"Do you like your room?" Henry asked. Owain swallowed and cleared his throat.

"Yes, it is very nice thank you," he said. "It is nice to sleep in a soft bed for a change instead of a cold stone floor."

The King smiled. "I am glad you like it," he said.

Owain felt Sir Stanley's eyes on him and turned to look at him. "Have we met?" he asked. Sir Stanley shook his head.

"No," he said. "I have met your brother Llywelyn though, and you reminded me of him." Owain was surprised. No one had ever said anything like that to him before. He didn't know what to make of it.

"In what way?" he asked.

"You look like him," Sir Stanley said.

"I have heard people say that a time or two," Owain agreed.

"It is more than that though. The way you carry yourself and the way you talk is similar as well. You both have an indefinable presence about you,"

Owain shrugged. "Thank you," he said unsure what else to say. He picked up a piece of fruit with two fingers and popped it into his mouth. He swallowed and picking up his cup took a sip of wine before turning his attention back to the knight. "How did you meet my brother?"

"He ambushed me with some men in my camp near the Gwynedd border." Sir Stanley explained.

Owain gave a small smile. "Well I can see you survived the encounter," he said.

"Yes, I did," Sir Stanley said with a smile of his own. "They put up a good fight though."

"I'm sure."

"Llywelyn did make it clear to me though that he will kill me the next time he sees me." He shuddered at the memory of the man's face as he told him of his fate the next time they met.

"I would take that to heart if I were you," Owain said. "My brother never says anything he doesn't mean."

"I believe it," Sir Stanley said picking up his cup and taking a sip of wine.

Owain picked up the bread and took a bite.

"Do you miss home Lord Owain?" Lord William asked. Owain finished chewing and swallowed before answering.

"Yes, very much," he said sounding very wistful. "I especially miss my family. They must have seen something in his face because suddenly they were all looking at him with sympathy. He felt very uncomfortable under their collective gazes.

"I understand," Lord William said softly.

"Will you be staying long with us, Lord Owain?" Lord Rosen asked. Owain turned to him relieved at the change of subject.

"I am not sure," he said taking another sip of wine. "The King has been nice enough to let me stay here for a time while I recover." He drained the last few drops of wine from his cup and popped the last piece of fruit into his mouth and chewed it thoughtfully.

"You may stay as long as you like," Henry said draining his cup.

Owain swallowed. "Thank you, Your Majesty," he said.

Henry smiled at him. "Have you thought any more about my proposal?" he asked.

Owain sighed inwardly. He had wondered how long it would take before the King brought that up. "In all honesty, Your Majesty, I have not. I have been too tired to think about much of anything," he said.

"I understand," Henry said. "Take your time. There is no rush."

"Thank you, Your Majesty." Owain picked up the decanter and refilled his cup. "This is an excellent wine," he said after taking a swallow.

"Do you eat like this back home, Lord Owain?" Lord William asked.

Owain shook his head. "No, I usually eat in my room back home," he said taking another sip of wine. "I think the last time I ate in the great hall with this many people my grandfather had just won a great victory and we were celebrating."

"Your grandfather was a great warrior in his day," Lord William agreed. "Is your uncle anything like him?"

Owain shook his head. "No, my uncle has never really shown himself to be anything like my grandfather," he said. "My father took after the old man more, and I see a lot of him in my brother Llywelyn as well."

"I know what you mean," Sir Stanley said. "I saw something of the man in your brother when I met him."

"What do you think of him as a leader?" Lord William asked.

Owain gave a bark of laughter. "He is not the kind of man that encourages people to follow him. I always thought it should have been my father who should have become ruler of Gwynedd after my grandfather's death, not my uncle," he said.

"I see," Henry said. He noticed once again Owain's disdain towards his uncle whenever he talked about the man. Clearly, there was no love lost between the two of them. He wondered how he could use this valuable bit of knowledge to his advantage. Owain drained his cup and placed it back on the table. Then he stood up and gave the King a small bow.

"This has been lovely, but I must go and rest. I am still very tired," he said turning to leave.

"Yes, of course," Henry said. "Do you need a guide, or can you find your own way back to your room?"

Owain shook his head. "No, I can find my way on my own." He turned then and left the hall.

Lord William shook his head in exasperation.

"He is very closed isn't he?" Lord Rosen observed.

"He's nervous," Sir Stanley said.

"Nervous of what?" Lord William asked.

"He is the only Welsh person in England in this castle, and I am guessing he has never been around this many English people at one time. Let alone ones that stared at him like that," he sympathized. "I felt the same way when I went to Aberfraw Castle to meet Prince Dafydd."

"I never thought of that," Lord William said abashedly.

"You wouldn't unless you had experienced the same thing yourself."

"Well said," Henry said with a smile. "I am sure he will become more comfortable in time." The rest nodded and went back to eating.

Owain walked through the halls looking for someone who could help him send his letter to his brother in Gwynedd. He had the sealed letter in his breast pocket and was eager to send it on its way. As he turned yet another corner he saw a young man in servant garb and waved to him. The man saw him and walked up to him, giving him a small bow of the head.

"Can I help you, My Lord?" he asked.

Owain nodded. "I have a letter that I want to send to my brother back in Gwynedd, Wales. Do you know anyone who can help me with that?" he asked.

The man nodded enthusiastically. "If you give it to me I can make sure it is sent out right away. There is a tinker that comes to the town once a month and he is due this afternoon. I believe he has gone to Gwynedd before, and I am sure he would take the letter for you," he said. Owain pulled the letter out of his breast pocket and handed it to the servant.

"Thank you," he said. The servant smiled.

"It is my pleasure, My Lord." He assured him. He slid the letter into his own pocket.

"Do you need help finding your room My Lord?"

"No, I am all right. Thank you." Owain turned then and went to find his room and get some rest. He was still exhausted despite a good night's sleep and an excellent breakfast. He suspected it would take a while for him to get his energy and his strength back after years of no exercise and poor living conditions. At least now he had warm clothes and good food to help him on his way to recovery. Even if they came, with a modicum of danger, he was well aware of the fact that he was deep in enemy territory here and needed to keep his wits about him at all times. But even though his body was weak from his years of imprisonment his mind was not. Unlike his father, he had been able to keep his mind from breaking through pure force of will and an absolute refusal to give in to fear and depression.

Aberfraw Castle, Clwyd Valley, Gwynedd, Wales Six weeks later...

Llywelyn sat in his room eating breakfast while Olan sat mending one of his wool tunics.

"You know it is a good thing that your clothing is so hardy, otherwise mending would be my full-time job," he said pulling the needle through the fabric for another stitch. Llywelyn laughed and took another mouthful of porridge. He had a second spoonful poised to put into his mouth when there was a knock on the door.

"Come in," he called and placed the spoon back in the bowl. The door opened, and the servant named Huw entered the room.

"My Lord, there is a letter for you from England," he said giving him a small bow of the head.

"Really?" Llywelyn said surprised. He couldn't think who would be writing to him from England. If the King had anything he wanted to say he would say it to Dafydd and not him. "Bring it here then."

Huw walked to him and placed the sealed letter in his hand. There was no signature on the outside, only his name and where he lived, and the seal was nothing special either. He broke it open and unfolding it was able to see who the letter was from. Seeing his brother's careful handwriting on the page gave him a strange feeling, part excitement to hear from him after so long, and part dread at what could have happened for him to be writing after four years of nothing. "Thank you for bringing this to me," he said.

"May I go now, My Lord?" Huw asked.

"Yes, take the remains of this breakfast to the kitchen."

"Yes, My Lord." Huw picked up the nearly empty bowl of porridge and left the room once more, shutting the door behind him as he left. Llywelyn opened the letter once more and began to read. Every word he read made him feel worse and by the end of the letter, he felt like his heart had been torn in two and someone had stomped on the pieces.

"What is wrong?" Olan asked seeing the look on his face. Llywelyn shook his head unable to talk from emotion. He held out the letter.

Olan stood up, and walking over to him took it from him. He walked back to his chair by the fire and opening the letter began to read it for himself. As he read he thought he could almost hear Owain's voice speaking...

Dear Llywelyn,

It feels strange writing this letter to you after so long. I am sorry I haven't kept in touch before, but they wouldn't let us have any contact with the outside world. I am writing to you to let you know that father has died.

It happened a few days ago. He was attempting to escape our tower cell when the makeshift rope snapped, and he fell and broke his neck. He died on impact, so he didn't suffer at all. I am sorry I have to tell you such sad news, but I wanted you to hear it from me first before it becomes public knowledge.

I thought you should also know that a few days after father's death the King of England came to my cell to release me from prison. He said that now that father is dead the treaty between England and Gwynedd is no longer valid, and so he didn't see any reason to keep me in prison anymore. He also made me a proposition to change sides and become a member of his court. He wants to start a civil war in Gwynedd and wants my help with it.

I told him I had to think about it. So I am staying here at Winchester Castle for the time being while I recover and slowly gain back the strength and energy I lost over the past four years of my imprisonment. While I stay here, I will try to get as much information as possible that might help our people if war does break out between the two lands. Give my best to mother and our brothers. I hope to be back with you all very soon.

Your affectionate brother,

Owain

Olan looked up from the letter and saw Llywelyn looking at him.

"I can't believe it," he said. "I just can't imagine a world that didn't include your father." Llywelyn nodded and cleared his suddenly dry throat.

"I know," he said, his voice cracking with grief.

"That proposal the King made to Owain sounds a little suspicious," Olan said picking up his mending once more.

"I know," Llywelyn agreed. "He didn't take the offer though which is something."

"Yes," Olan agreed, pulling the needle through the fabric for a final stitch and tying it off. "Are you going to show your mother the letter?"

Llywelyn sighed. "I don't really see that I have a choice. I would rather she hear it firsthand than second," he said. He stood up then and stretched. "I think I will go now and see her."

Olan put aside the mended tunic and stood up as well. He handed Llewelyn the letter to and gave him an encouraging smile.

"Give your mother my best. This won't be easy on her. I know they were very close," he said.

"Yes, they were," Llywelyn agreed.

Olan reached out and patted him on the shoulder.

Llywelyn managed a small smile of appreciation before turning and leaving the room to find his mother.

Chapter 10

A Declaration of War

As Llywelyn walked down the hall to his mother's room, he thought about how much his parents had meant to each other. From everything he had been told, their marriage had been one of love and mutual respect. Caradog ap Tomas had been a noble and had been the Lord of Anglesey. But that had not been why they had married. He had only seen his grandfather Caradog a few times when he was a child. He had died before Llywelyn had left for warrior training at the age of 13.

He reached his mother's room and knocked twice.

"Come in." He heard his mother call from inside the room. Turning the handle he opened the door and walked into the room. His mother was sitting by the fire embroidering a piece of cloth that covered her lap and trailed down onto the floor. She looked up as he entered the room and smiled when she saw him. He smiled back but he felt his lips tremble with the effort.

"Llywelyn, it is good to see you," she said. He felt sick. How could he tell her? She had barely been holding on these last four years, clinging on to the vague hope that she would see her love again. He shook himself mentally and feeling like the harbinger of doom walked further into the room.

"Hello mother," he said. Now that he was closer she could see the shellshock look on his face.

"What's wrong? What has happened?" she asked concerned. He said nothing, but simply placed his hand in his pocket and pulled out Owain's letter. He handed it mutely to her and stood watching her as she opened it and began to read. He saw her face change as she read Owain's words. By the time she reached the end of the page, she was crying freely but silently. He walked around the back of her chair and hugged her from behind as she wept. He tried to give her some of his strength. Breathing slowly, he managed to hide his emotions behind what he hoped was a blank face in order to be strong for her. He could break down later in private.

"I am so sorry," he said letting go and walking back around to the front of her chair to face her. She wiped her eyes with her sleeve and attempted to pull herself together.

"I am sorry for us all," she said in a voice cracked with emotion.

"Are you going to be all right?" he asked walking over to the second chair by the fire. He sat down facing his mother.

"I will be in time," she said giving him a watery smile. He smiled back at her in turn. "Have you showed this letter to Dafydd yet?" He shook his head.

"Not yet. I wanted you to see it first," he said.

"Thank you for that. But I do think you need to show him this letter. It changes everything," she said.

"I know," he said.

"Your uncle has been looking for a way to get out of that treaty for a long time, and now it looks like he gets his wish," Llywelyn smiled.

"I highly doubt he wished for something like this," he said.

Sanena nodded her head in agreement. "No, I don't think so either. I think you need to show him this letter sooner rather than later. We don't know how long Owain can string the King along for," she said.

"You are right," he said. "If you think you will be all right on your own for a bit, I think I will go and take it to Dafydd now." He stood up then and walking over to her gave his mother another quick hug. She smiled at him.

"I will be fine. Go and see him," she said.

"All right then. I will see you later." He turned then and left the room once more.

Sanena sat and thought about her husband. In all reality, he had been dead for years. She had never let herself admit it to anyone, but she had known the day she watched him being taken away that she would never see him again this side of the grave. At least she still had her sons. Llywelyn had truly become his father's son now, and it filled her heart with pride to see him thriving in his new role as head warrior. She lay down her embroidering and stood up. She smoothed down her skirts then and went to find something to drink. She suddenly felt in need of a good stiff drink.

Llywelyn found Dafydd in the great hall finishing his breakfast. Dafydd turned his head at the sound of the door opening and seeing who it was waved. Llywelyn walked up to the table.

"Ah, Llywelyn, how are you?" Dafydd asked with a smile that disappeared when he saw the look on his face. Llywelyn didn't say anything. He pulled the letter from his pocket and laid it on the table beside Dafydd's plate.

"I got that this morning," he said. He pulled out a chair and sat down.

"What is this?" Dafydd asked picking up the letter in two fingers.

"It is a letter from my brother, Owain," Llywelyn explained. "He wrote it from Winchester Castle where he is currently residing."

Dafydd shook his head in confusion. "I don't understand. He is supposed to be in prison in The Tower of London."

"He explains everything in the letter," Llywelyn said picking up the brandy decanter and pouring himself a cup. He took a long swallow and instantly felt better as he felt it warm his insides. It wasn't until he stopped shivering that he realized he had been doing so ever since he had read his brother's words. It must be nerves he decided.

Dafydd opened the letter and began to read. Llywelyn watched his face as he read. It was a much different picture than he had seen on his mother's face only a short time before. Instead of breaking down in tears, he watched as his uncle grew angrier and angrier with every word he read. When he reached the end of the page he threw the letter back onto the table with such force that he made his plate jump. Taking a deep breath he attempted to control his emotions enough to speak.

"Thank you for bringing this to me," he said a little breathlessly.

"I thought you needed to see it," Llywelyn said taking another sip of brandy.

"Thank you," Dafydd said again.

"This changes everything doesn't it?"

"Yes, everything," Dafydd agreed.

"What are you going to do?" Llywelyn asked curiously.

"I am not doing anything. The King has done it all for me," Dafydd explained.

"What do you mean?"

"Now that I am no longer held by the bounds of that treaty I am going to do what I should have done years ago."

"And that would be what exactly?"

"I am going to declare war on England and rid us of them for good." Llywelyn smiled and Dafydd smiled back.

"What will be my role in this?"

"Come to my room later and we can go over it all then." Llywelyn nodded his understanding. Then he drained his cup and stood up to leave.

"This plan of yours sounds like something grandfather would have done," he said.

Dafydd grinned. "Well maybe it is time I take a page from the old man's book," he said. The two men clasped hands then for the first time ever and then let go. Llywelyn turned then and left the hall once more.

Llywelyn made his way back to his room with thoughts of battle strategy in his head. He didn't know what role he would play in this war, but he suspected it would probably involve some scouting. He reached his room and walked inside. Olan wasn't there. He crossed to the fireplace and kneeling laid another piece of wood on the fire and watched as it took and sent sparks flying upward.

He stood up then and went over to his closet to take an inventory of the clothing he owned. As he stood counting tunics, leggings, and every other kind of clothing he possessed, he heard the door open and turned his head to see Olan entering the room.

"There you are," he said.

"How did it go with your mother?" Olan asked as he walked over to the fire and laid an armload of wood into the basket beside the hearth.

"She was very upset."

"I can imagine," Olan said laying yet another piece of wood on the fire and making it roar.

"My uncle's reaction was a bit surprising, however."

"Oh?" Olan prompted.

"Well, first he got really mad to the point where he couldn't speak," Llywelyn explained.

"Understandable," Olan said standing up and dusting off the knees of his wool leggings.

"Well, then he said that because the treaty is broken he is going to do what he should have done years ago and is going to declare war on England to rid us of them forever."

Olan was shocked. He never thought Dafydd would have the guts to do something so bold as to declare war on the English crown.

"Wow," he said.

"I know," Llywelyn agreed.

"What will your role be in this?"

"I am not sure yet. I have to go to his room later and discuss it with him."

"Who would have thought a few simple words on a page would provoke such momentous actions," Olan said.

Llywelyn nodded his head in agreement. "I know," he said again. "I am trying to figure out if I have enough clothing for all of this, and I need to find my armor as well."

"That is packed away. I will go and get it for you. It will need polishing," Olan said.

"Thank you." Olan turned and left the room, leaving Llywelyn alone once more with his thoughts.

Llywelyn stared into the fire and thought about his father and his grandfather and what they would have thought about what his uncle was proposing to do. He thought his grandfather would have approved. He had meant it when he told Dafydd that this plan sounded like something his grandfather would have done. He thought that maybe his father would have approved as well. He wished they were both here now to help guide his uncle. He was afraid Dafydd wasn't quite up to the task of leading an army to war. He had never been one for battle and so had spent more time with matters of state than on the battlefield like his father and grandfather before him.

But maybe he wasn't giving the man enough credit. He had done well as a ruler so far.

A few hours later he went to find Dafydd in his room. He was alone in his room and seemed relieved to see him as he walked in the door.

"Please, sit," he said.

Llywelyn sat down by the fire and turned his chair to face his uncle. "So, have you decided what my role in this should be?" he asked. Dafydd nodded.

"I have sent my message to England. It won't get there for at least a month, but in the meantime, I will need to start collecting the troops. I would like your help with that. Then I will need you to do some scouting for me," Dafydd said.

"All right," Llywelyn said.

"As soon as the troops are assembled, we will start out. I said in my message that I will meet their troops somewhere in the middle of Gwynedd because I want to keep the fighting away from the people as much as possible."

"Good idea."

"Once you have ascertained when Henry's troops are up to, come and find me."

"I will do that. What about when the fighting starts?"

"I want you at the head of the army with me and Captain Carrol where you belong as head warrior." Llywelyn nodded.

"Is that all?" he asked.

"Yes, I think so," Dafydd said.

"All right then," Llywelyn said standing up. He turned then and left the room once more.

Chapter 11

The Preparation of War

Meanwhile, Sanena went looking for her two youngest sons to tell them of their father's death. Her heart was heavy as she searched for them. How was she going to tell them that their father was gone and never coming back? Gruffudd had loved all of his sons equally; he had always tried to give attention to each of them in turn. He had been a good father and now he was gone forever from all of their lives.

Her footsteps sounded hollow to her ears as she walked through the halls of the castle, searching for her sons. As she passed different rooms, she would stick her head in the doorways to see if she could see them. But they didn't seem to be anywhere in the castle. She walked to the front doors, motioning for the guard on the inside of the doors to open them. He nodded and opened the doors for her. She smiled at him in thanks and walked through into the courtyard beyond.

She found her sons in the center of the courtyard, taking turns shooting an arrow at a man they had made out of straw that sat a short distance away. Rhodri had the bow now and sent an arrow directly into the center of the straw man and laughed at his success. Despite her sorrow at the loss of her husband, she couldn't help smiling to herself at her youngest son's prowess with the bow. He was growing up so nicely. Soon he would be ready for his first sword. Up until this point, he had only been permitted to use wooden swords while he learned the art of a swordsman. His birthday was coming soon, and shortly before his last mission before he had been arrested and sent to England, Gruffudd had commissioned a small sword to be made for Rhodri for his birthday. Getting your first sword was usually a very special event, but now that his father was gone it would be even more precious.

"Good shot," Dafydd said encouragingly to his little brother. "That would have been a nasty stomach wound. Why don't you try again?" He handed Rhodri another arrow and watched as he pulled the string back to his cheek and let the arrow fly. It hit the straw man right where the forehead would have been. Rhodri laughed with pleasure at his success.

"Well done, Rhodri," Sanena said as she walked up to them. They both turned around and saw her walking towards them with a smile on her face.

"Hello mother," Dafydd said.

"Hello, boys. Having fun?" They nodded their heads in reply. Rhodri handed Dafydd the bow. He fitted an arrow to the string and hit the straw man directly where the heart would have been.

"Great shot," Rhodri said excitedly.

"Thanks," Dafydd said lowering the bow to the ground. He walked over and pulled the arrows from the target and placed them back in the quiver.

"Boys, there is something I need to tell you," she said softly.

"What is it?" Dafydd asked walking back to where he had left the bow and picking it up once more.

"Llywelyn received a letter this morning from your brother Owain in England saying that your father died several weeks ago while attempting to escape from their tower cell in The Tower of London where they were being held." The two boys stared at her with twin looks of bewilderment on their faces.

"I don't understand," Rhodri said. "How can our father be dead?"

"Good question," Dafydd agreed.

"The makeshift rope he was using snapped and he fell and broke his neck," she explained.

"So he is gone, just like that?" Rhodri said.

"I know it is hard to believe, but it is the truth. Your father is gone, and he isn't coming back," she said.

"So he is really gone?" Rhodri asked almost pleadingly. She looked at him with sympathy.

"Yes," she said softly. "I am so sorry boys." A single tear leaked from her eyes and slid down her face followed shortly by a second. Dafydd walked over to her and placed the bow in her hand.

"Come and shoot with us. It will make you feel better," he said.

She smiled at him. "All right. What do I do?"

"Here, I will show you." He showed her how to hold the bow and how to set the arrow to the string. Then he showed her how to pull the string back to her cheek, and watched as she let the string go and sent the arrow flying straight into the straw man at the point where his forehead would be.

"Nice shot," Both boys said together and laughed.

She smiled at her success and felt their joy. Dafydd handed her a second arrow and watched as she fitted it to the string and pulling the string to her cheek let loose the arrow and hit the straw man at the point where the neck would be. They all laughed then, and feeling a little lighter she took a third arrow from her son and let it fly.

The next morning Llywelyn woke early. The fire had gone out in the night and so the room was ice cold. He got out of bed and dressed quickly. He walked over to the window and opening the shutters looked out of it to try and judge the weather for the day. He saw a couple of large dark clouds hanging in the sky heavy with rain. He shut the shutters once more and walked back to his bed. Sitting down on it, he put on his riding boots, the ones that were lined with fur, and pulled on his thick wool traveling cloak, which had a nice thick hood. Feeling ready to face the outdoors he walked to the door, and opening it left the room.

Out in the hall, he stopped for a moment while he tried to decide whether to go and try and grab a bite from the kitchen before leaving or wait until he reached the town to eat something at one of the taverns there. The thought of a cup of nice dark beer with his breakfast sounded like the best idea. He thought he should find

Talia before he left though and leave a message with her for Olan. On that thought, he started walking down the hall in search of the lass.

It didn't take long, however. As he turned the corner a few moments later, he found Talia walking towards him, carrying a heavy laden tray in her arms. She started with surprise seeing him and stopped in her tracks.

"Hello there, Talia. Is that for my mother?" he asked pointing to the tray she was carrying.

She nodded. "Yes. I am just taking Lady Sanena her breakfast. Are you going somewhere, My Lord?" she asked seeing that he was dressed for travel.

"I am going into the town today to find someone," he said.

"Oh."

"I was looking for you because I wanted to leave a message for Olan," he said.

"What's the message?" she asked. Her face had lightened with the thought of her love.

"Just let him know if you see him that I don't need him today so he can take the day off. I will probably be gone all day. I don't know how long it will take to find the person I am looking for. Tell him I will see him tonight when I get back." She nodded.

"Yes, of course, My Lord," she said.

"Thank you," he said. He made to go past her when he stopped. "You know I am really happy you two got together. I don't think I have ever seen him so happy."

"Thank you, My Lord," she said with a shy smile. He smiled back and started off down the hall towards the front doors.

A little while later, as he was riding down the road to the town, he thought about Olan and his happiness in his relationship with Talia. He had meant what he said. He was incredibly happy for his old friend. He wondered if he would ever find happiness with someone the way Olan had. It didn't seem likely. Not with the kind of job he was doing, and in any case he was royalty and so he couldn't just marry whomever he liked. It would have to be someone of noble birth, and all the girls he had met in his work for his uncle had either been young and irritating or otherwise older and just out for his money and prestige. He shook himself mentally. Not every girl would be like that. Maybe one day he would meet a nice young woman who liked him for himself and was politically connected enough to pass as a suitable match for someone in his position.

As he reached the town, he headed straight for the tavern. He was starving and wanted nothing more than a good hot meal accompanied by a cup of cold dark beer to wash it all down. From what he remembered his father saying, Carrol, the Captain of the Royal Army liked to frequent both the tavern and the inn in town and he highly doubted the man would have changed his habits at all over the past four years which meant that the proprietor of the tavern would most likely know who he was and just perhaps where he lived as well. It was a start in any case.

He reached the tavern, and dismounting tied his horse's reins to the doorpost. Then he walked to the door and pushed it open. The moment he walked inside he was hit with the smells of heavy pipe smoke mixed with the sweet smell of hops and the milder smell of food. The pipe smoke was so thick in the air he almost couldn't see the inhabitancy of the room, and the smell of the hops was heavy on his lungs.

All eyes were on him as he walked up to the bar. The barman took a double-take when he saw Llywelyn. He cleared his throat and shook his head. "My Lord, what are you doing here?" he asked. He was a small man with a pointed chin and small beady dark eyes fringed with long lashes that seemed to water from the pipe smoke that hung in the air.

"I am looking for someone," Llywelyn explained.

"I see," the barman said slowly.

"I am looking for a Captain Carrol of the Royal Army. I was told he frequents this tavern from time to time." The barman nodded.

"Yes, he does," he confirmed.

"Has he been in here recently?"

"He is here now," the barman said pointing to a table in the back of the room closest to the fire. Llywelyn turned his head and saw a man sitting alone at the table drinking a cup of beer.

"Thank you," he said.

"Can I get you anything, My Lord?"

Llywelyn nodded. "I'm starving," he said.

"We have a good special on at the moment," the man said.

"I will have a big plate of it then, and a pint of your beer, please."

"Coming right up."

Llywelyn pulled some coins from his pocket and slid them across the bar. The barman picked them up and dropped them into a cashbox that sat behind the counter. Then he turned and walked through a door into what Llywelyn assumed must be the kitchen due to the smell of cooking that wafted through the door when it was opened.

Llywelyn began to wind his way through the tables until he reached the one where Captain Carrol sat drinking alone. He looked up as Llywelyn reached him and started in surprise.

"My Lord, what are you doing here? You are extremely far from the castle." Llywelyn smiled and took the seat opposite him.

"I was looking for you," he said. The man didn't look any different than the last time he had seen him. He was not much shorter than himself and had short wavy dirty blond hair that seemed to stick out in all directions and framed a thin face with large emerald green eyes and a small snubbed nose. He had a large scar that ran down one side of his face that made him look fierce with his large muscular frame and arms that looked like small tree trunks he was the image of a soldier.

"Well, what can I help you with?" he asked picking up his beer and taking a swallow.

"Well," Llywelyn started, but just then a pretty young woman with long light-brown hair and startlingly bright blue eyes walked up to the table and lay a plate in front of him piled high with food and a large pint of beer.

"Your meal and beer, My Lord," she said a little shyly. He smiled at her which made her blush.

"Thank you," he said. She bobbed her head in response and sped away back through the tables.

Carrol laughed. "She liked you," he said grinning.

"Thanks," Llywelyn said. He took a swallow of beer and cleared his throat. "The reason I came to find you is to tell you about my uncle's new plans," he said stabbing his fork into a sausage and taking a large bite.

"I didn't know he had any," Carrol said looking longingly at his plate of food. Llywelyn saw him looking and smiled at him.

"Here, have a sausage," he said.

Carrol nodded his thanks and picking one up with two fingers popped it whole into his mouth. Llywelyn finished his own and took another swig of beer. "So, what is the Prince planning then?" Carrol asked when he had swallowed.

"I received a letter from my brother in England yesterday and it has changed things a bit."

"Really? What did it say?"

"Here, you can read it for yourself," Llywelyn said pulling the letter from his breast pocket and handing it across the table to him. Carrol took it and began to read. Llywelyn continued to eat his way through his breakfast while he waited for the captain to finish reading. He was almost through his plate when Carrol skillfully placed the letter back on the table and turned to look at him.

"So, what is the Prince planning to do?" he asked.

"He is going to declare war on the King. He wants to rid our land forever of the English bastards," Llywelyn said taking another swig of beer.

"That is only fitting," Carrol said taking a sip from his cup. "So where do we fit into the picture then?"

"As head warrior, I have been set with the task of organizing the troops, and then I am to go and scout for the army," Llywelyn said biting into a piece of fruit.

"I see."

Llywelyn finished chewing and then swallowed. "I could use your help though. I don't know who half the troops are, and in any case, they don't know me yet. They are much more likely to listen to you," he said.

"Very true," Carrol agreed.

"Thank you. Also while I am off scouting the Prince will need to have someone to help him with battle tactics and all that. He is much more a statesman than a warrior."

Carrol nodded. "I can do that," he said.

Llywelyn smiled. "Good," he said.

"Well, shall we go and get started?" Llywelyn nodded and downing the last of his beer stood up. Carrol followed and they left the tavern together.

That same afternoon a messenger rode out of the gates of Aberfraw castle and rode off in the direction of England carrying with him the sealed message from Dafydd for the King. Llywelyn and Carrol spent the next several weeks gathering the troops and preparing them for battle. Llywelyn fell into bed each night exhausted from the day's training session. The men were working hard though, and he was pleased to see the progress they were making. He was happy to have Carrol by his side. He had been right about the men having a hard time taking him seriously. They listened much better to the older man than they did to himself.

One day while they were training, Dafydd came out to watch and was shocked to see the progress they had made. He congratulated both Llywelyn and Carrol on their leadership and their ability to work together so well.

"This kind of cooperation will make all the difference," he said. The two men nodded their heads in agreement.

"It is all part of warrior training, My Prince," Carrol explained. "If you can't cooperate with others and take orders then you are no good as a soldier."

"That makes sense," Dafydd said. He turned to Llywelyn then. "The message should have reached the King by now. I will need you to start soon for the northern border."

Llywelyn nodded. "I will need a few days to prepare," he said.

"How long?"

"At least three days to gather supplies and pack."

"Very well," Dafydd said. "Let us all have supper together in the great hall tonight to celebrate your success with the men here."

"That would be lovely, thank you, My Prince," Carrol said pleased. Llywelyn nodded in agreement.

"Very good," Dafydd said, and with that left them alone once more to finish training for the day.

Three days later, Llywelyn walked into the stables carrying a couple of saddlebags filled to bursting with supplies. Olan was already in the stables preparing the horses for travel. He was just finishing cinching up Arling's cinch on her saddle when Llywelyn entered the stable. Seeing him he smiled and walked over to him. He took two of the saddlebags and went to buckle them onto his own horse's saddle. Llywelyn saw that Olan had already buckled his sword on to the saddle. His bow and arrows were in one of the saddlebags that he held in his hands. He buckled the bags on behind his sword and checked to make sure they were secure. Then he mounted up and turned to see Olan doing the same. Then he clicked his tongue and rode out of the stables followed by Olan.

They rode to the front gates and were waved through by the guard on duty who gave them a courteous nod as they passed. Llywelyn nodded back and smiled. Then once they were through the gates, they gave their horses a light kick and galloped off into the distance. Llywelyn took one look back to take one last look at the castle. He didn't know how long it would be before he saw it again. Then he turned his head back to the front as they rode out of sight. He hoped that his family would be all right, his mother and brothers. He couldn't imagine how Olan was feeling leaving Talia like this and not knowing when he would see her again. For that reason alone he was glad he didn't have anyone. He didn't know if he could leave like this if he had a great love. He shook himself and tried to focus on the task ahead. There was a war about to begin, and he was going to be an integral part of it. He should be happy for the honor of the position his uncle had given to him. So why then did he feel so uneasy?

Chapter 12

A Council of War

Winchester Castle, Chester, England

Three weeks later...

The messenger from Aberfraw Castle reached Winchester Castle. He had ridden hard and fast to reach the castle as quickly as possible so he could get the job over with and get back to Gwynedd where he felt safe. He was constantly looking over his shoulder waiting for an attack that he was certain would come.

As he rode up to the castle he was hailed by the guard on the front gates.

"Stop there and state your purpose," the guard demanded. The messenger nodded his head in understanding and cleared his throat.

"I am a messenger from Aberfraw Castle in the Valley of Clwyd Gwynedd, Wales, and I have a message to your King from Prince Dafydd of Gwynedd," he said.

"You may enter," the guard said and opened the gates. The messenger rode through into the courtyard beyond. He dismounted and a stable boy took his horse off towards the stables. He walked up to the front doors of the castle, which were opened for him by another guard who gave him a nod of greeting. He nodded back and walked through.

The moment he entered the great hall he was shocked to see just how large the place was. The entrance hall alone was 10 times larger than that of Aberfraw, and twice as grand with its high ceilings, and what looked like marble floors. He wondered if the rest of the castle was just as grand. He felt extremely uncomfortable and wished someone would come along soon.

After what felt like an eternity, a young man in a servant's uniform saw him standing there and walked towards him.

"May I help you?" the man asked. He was a short man with a kind round face and long-lashed soft gray eyes.

The messenger nodded eagerly. "Yes," he said. "I have come from Aberfraw Castle in the valley of Clwyd Gwynedd, Wales with a message for your King from Prince Dafydd, the ruler of Gwynedd."

"The King is a bit busy at the moment," the servant said.

"Oh," the messenger said disappointedly.

"If you give me your message, I can give it to him when he is free," the servant said encouragingly. His mood perked up at these words. Maybe if he gave his message to this young man he could go and find something to eat and a place to rest for the night before heading back the next day. He nodded his head in agreement.

"All right," he said reaching into his pocket. He pulled out the sealed message and handed it to the young man. The servant took it and slid it into his breast pocket in turn.

"I will make sure the King gets this the moment he is free," he said. The messenger nodded.

"Thank you," he said and turning left the castle.

He found the stables and slipped a coin to the stable boy in payment for looking after his horse for him.

"Do you know of any good places to stay in the town?" he asked the lad.

"There is an excellent inn right in the center of the town. I would stay there if I were you. They always have good food and their beer is to die for. Or so I have heard," the young man said.

"Thank you," he said. He mounted up then, and the young man handed him his reins. Then he rode out of the stables. The guard at the gate seemed surprised to see him leaving so soon after arriving.

"Leaving so soon?" he asked. He nodded in reply and rode through the open gate. Then he turned his horse's head in the direction of the town and rode off in that direction.

The King was sitting in the dining hall eating an early supper when the young servant came to find him and deliver Dafydd's message. He walked up to the King and gave a small bow.

"Your Majesty, there is a message for you from Prince Dafydd of Gwynedd, Wales," he said pulling the sealed message from his pocket. He placed it on the table beside the King's plate and gave another small bow.

Henry picked it up and broke the seal with his knife. Then folding it open quickly read it through. He reached the bottom of the message and looked up at the servant. "Where did you get this?" he asked.

"A messenger from Aberfraw Castle brought it just now," the young man explained.

"Did he give you any other messages for me?"

"No, Your Majesty."

"Very well, you may go."

"Thank you, Your Majesty." The young servant turned then and left the hall once more.

"Is everything all right?" Lord William asked. He sat to the King's left as he always did. He was a creature of habit and didn't see any reason to change. Henry said nothing. He simply picked up the note and handed it to his friend. Then he picked up his goblet of wine and took a long swallow to calm his nerves. The message had unnerved him more than he was letting on. In fact, it had shaken him to the core but he would never tell.

Lord William unfolded the message and began to read. The King watched his face change from mild curiosity to outright indignation as he read farther and farther down the page. By the time he reached the bottom of the message, his face was bright red with rage, and he dropped the piece of paper like it was a hot coal that had burnt his fingers.

Henry smiled at his friend's reaction. It made him feel a little better.

"What is he playing at?" Lord William demanded hotly.

"I don't think he is playing," Henry said picking up his goblet once more and draining it. Then he picked up the decanter and refilled it and took another healthy swallow of the sweet wine.

"He states in his message that his brother's death could have been avoided if we had taken care of him properly," Lord William said with a snort of indignation.

"Lord Owain did reveal to me what they were given to eat, and I saw the conditions they were living in. They would have driven anyone to such desperate measures in the end," Henry said picking up a piece of bread and biting into it.

"Then why is Lord Owain not dead as well?"

"I don't know. A stronger constitution I suppose," Henry said taking another bite of bread.

Lord William shook his head. "What are we going to do about this?" he asked.

Henry sighed and took another sip of wine. Then he placed his goblet back on the table and wiped his lips with the back of his hand and cleared his throat. "I don't see any other choice than to answer his call to war," Lord William nodded in agreement.

"No, I don't see any other choice either," he said.

"I need you to find Lord Rosen, Lord Edmond, and Sir Stanley and bring them to the council chamber. We need to have a meeting about this."

"I will go right now," Lord William said standing up.

"Oh, and find my son Edward; he should be a part of this meeting as well."

"Are you going to send him to war?"

"Yes. It is time he is given some responsibility," Lord William nodded.

"I understand. I will go and find him and the others and meet you in the council chamber shortly," he said and with a small bow of the head to the King left the hall.

Henry finished his wine while he thought about Dafydd's message. Then he put down his empty goblet and standing up left the hall.

About an hour later, he was joined in the council chamber by all the members of the royal council to discuss Dafydd's message. Lord William had managed to find his son Edward as well and had brought him along as the King had requested. The various members sat around him at the table. Lord William in his customary spot on the King's left, and Sir Stanley on his right and beside him sat the Prince. Across the table sat Lord Rosen, and Lord Edmond both with identical looks of curiosity on their faces. Sir Stanley however kept an impassive face while he waited to hear what the King had to say.

Henry looked at his son with apprehension. He didn't know if he was quite up to the task of leading the whole of the English army into battle. But how would he learn if he wasn't given the chance to try? He knew he had to let him spread his wings so to speak and find out who he truly was as both a man and as a leader. It was a difficult thing to do as a father to send his son and heir off to battle knowing that he might not come back. But it was the way, and he couldn't change that fact. Edward had grown to be a handsome young man with a good head on his shoulders. He reminded him a lot of himself at his age. He shook himself mentally and cleared his throat.

"I suppose you are all wondering why I have called this emergency meeting?"

"Lord William didn't say much other than you wanted to see us," Lord Rosen said.

"Well, the reason I have called you all here is to share with you a message that I received from Gwynedd, Wales and to discuss what needs to be done." They all nodded in understanding. He reached into his pocket and pulled out Dafydd's message and handed it to Sir Stanley. He watched as each person's face changed as he read the message. It made him feel better about his decision to see them all so angry at the Prince's written words.

After several minutes had passed, and everyone at the table had read the message they all looked to the King to hear what he had to say.

"What are we going to do about this?" Lord Rosen demanded.

"I have no choice but to answer the call to war. I will need all of your help to come up with the best battle plan as possible before I answer his call to arms," Henry said. They all nodded in universal agreement. He turned to look at his son and saw not anger on his face, but fear. He saw his father looking and quickly tried to hide it. But he had seen it all the same. He wished he could tell his son that everything would be all right and that he had nothing to fear. But that would be a lie.

Owain meanwhile was walking down the hall in search of something to eat when he heard the King's voice coming from inside the council chamber as he passed. Curious, he stopped in his tracks and put his ear to the crack between the wall and the door to listen.

"I agree," Lord Rosen said. "We can not let this go unanswered." Owain shook his head in confusion and pressed his entire body against the door in order to get his ear as close to the crack as possible.

"Lord Dafydd is a fool if he thinks we will not come at him with our full force," Lord Edmond said.

"I met with the man four years ago, and he didn't seem a fool to me," Sir Stanley said.

"Then we are all agreed," the King said. "We will answer his call to war." Owain felt his stomach give a violent twinge at what he had just heard. If the King had received a message from Dafydd calling him out to war, then clearly, he had read his letter. He felt sick. The whole point he had been trying to make by sending that letter was to keep the two lands from going to war. It was clear by what he had just heard that Dafydd had taken his words out of context and was using them to his own aims.

"What will be my role in this?" asked a voice he didn't recognize.

"I want you to lead the army," the King said.

"But father, that is what you should be doing, not me. Father?"

Owain wondered who on earth this could be.

"I am too old and too tired to lead them anymore. Besides, you are my son and heir and it is time you tested your strengths as a leader."

"Are you sure about this?" Edward asked.

"You will not be alone. You will have Lord Edmond and Sir Stanley at your side, and you couldn't ask for two better companions in battle."

"Don't worry, Your Majesty, we will take good care of him," Sir Stanley said reassuringly.

"What do you have to say about this Lord Edmond?" the King asked.

"We should send the foot soldiers on ahead because they are slower, and then send the cavalry on afterward," Lord Edmond said.

"I agree," Sir Stanley chimed in.

"Should I go along as well to support the Prince, Your Majesty," Lord William asked.

"No, that won't be necessary," the King replied.

Owain had heard enough. Feeling shaky with a mixture of excitement and trepidation he turned and started back down the hall in the direction of his room. It was time to go and find his brother and prepare the Welsh army for what was coming.

Chapter 13

Brothers Reunited

The border between Gwynedd and England, Gwynedd, Wales

One month later...

It was early evening when Llywelyn and Olan sat on their horses atop a hill that looked down upon the English army spread out below. The air was damp from the rain the night before. It was hard to imagine how the English soldiers below kept their fires going in the damp out in the open like that. At least they had the common sense to camp in the woods where it was somewhat dry Llywelyn thought. Even at this height, they could still smell the smoke from their fires which spoke to him of how clueless they were. Wet wood equaled smoky fires which produced little heat. Just barely enough to cook on, but not enough to keep a man warm.

They could hear the braying of mules and the neighing of horses in the distance. The sounds were making Arling toss her head every so often in agitation. He didn't blame her. This was not a sight he was happy to see. It made him uneasy to see the vastness of the army spread out below, and he was certain that this was only a small portion of the King's army. It was clear to him that they were more than a match for the Welsh army.

"Do you think that is the whole of the English army down there?" Olan asked as if reading his thoughts.

"No. I don't see a command tent down there and I am sure the King would have one."

"Do you really think the King is someone who would fight his own battles?"

Llywelyn smiled. "I don't know," he said with a laugh in his voice. "In any case, I don't see any sign of command down there. I think it is just a regiment of foot soldiers we are seeing."

"I see horses and a couple of mules in the distance," Olan said pointing.

Llywelyn nodded. "Pack mules and horses to pull the supply wagons," he said.

"What do you want to do?"

"I saw a clearing a few miles back down the road," Llywelyn said. "We can camp there for the night and then go to find Dafydd and the Welsh army in the morning." Olan nodded his head in agreement. They gave their horses a light kick and rode off back down the road the way they had come.

Meanwhile, Owain was making his slow way on foot through the woods. His horse had bucked him off a few days back when she heard one of the horses in the English camp call out and he had been on foot ever since. Feeling somewhat vulnerable without a horse to make a quick getaway he had been sticking to the woods to stay out of sight of the English. He was sure that his absence had been noticed by now.

He was surprised to see just how far the English army had come in just one month. Granted it was only the foot soldiers, but they had still come on rather quickly for a bunch of men on foot accompanied by pack mules and horse-drawn supply wagons. He knew from what he had overheard that now the foot soldiers were on the Gwynedd side of the border; they would wait in their camp until the cavalry reached them before moving on to meet the Welsh army in battle. Before he had left he had written everything he had heard down and brought it with him buried deep in the pocket of the cloak the King had given him when he had first come to Winchester Castle. He intended to give it to his brother whenever he found him.

Llywelyn and Olan reached the forest clearing a short time later and dismounted.

"Take care of the horses," Llywelyn said. "I will go and find some wood for a fire." He turned then and walked off into the trees. Olan began untacking the horses and hobbling them for the night. Then he took all the saddlebags and laid them together under a tree for safekeeping. He felt unsettled in his mind as he collected rocks and began to build a fire ring. He knew it was the sight of the English army on the Gwynedd side of the border. He had managed until now to think of the war as an abstract idea, but after what he had just seen he now had to admit to himself that it was all real.

Llywelyn returned a short time later carrying an armload of wood. Seeing that Olan had already built up a fire ring he dropped the wood beside it and kneeling began to make up the fire. Olan pulled the flint and steel from one of the saddlebags and walked over to the fire. He knelt beside Llywelyn and began the process of lighting the wood stacked there. In just a few strikes of the flint and steel, the fire roared to life. Llywelyn smiled to himself to see little to no smoke as the flames rose skyward.

"I think I will go and find some water, and maybe see if I can catch us some fish for supper," Olan said standing up.

"Good idea," Llywelyn said stretching out his legs with a sigh of contentment.

Olan pulled water skins and a kettle from the saddlebags as well as a fishing line. Then he turned and headed off through the trees to find a stream of some kind. He found a stream not too far from the clearing and kneeling began to fill the water skins and kettle. Then he plucked a couple of hairs from his head and threaded them onto the hook at the end of the fishing line and cast it into the water. After a minute or so, he felt a tug on the line and pulling it in saw that he had caught a nice fat fish on the end of it. He tossed it out of the water and killed it swiftly with a rock. Then he cast his line into the stream once more.

Owain fought his way through the dense undergrowth and found himself on the bank of a stream—the same stream where Olan sat a short distance away casting his fishing line time and time again as he collected several fish for his and Llywelyn's supper that evening. Owain knelt down and drank thirstily from the stream.

His feet were killing him from walking for days, and he wanted nothing more than to take off his boots and put his feet in the water. He was about to do so when he heard a noise. He listened again and realized it was someone humming. He stood up very carefully in order not to make any noise and crept quietly in the direction of the sound. After only a short distance, he saw the figure of a man hunched over by the edge of the stream and crept around behind the figure to have the element of surprise.

Olan had finished collecting enough fish for a good size meal and had knelt to take a drink from the stream before heading back. He was about to sit back up when he felt a hand come around his throat from behind and froze.

"Tell me your name and who you work for or I will slit your throat," Owain said in a quiet voice. Olan was confused. He thought that he recognized the voice, but he couldn't be sure. He tried to speak around his racing pulse. "My name is Olan. I am companion to Lord Llywelyn of Aberfraw Castle, in the valley of Clwyd," he said a little breathlessly. Owain released him and he sat up panting a little. He took a few deep breaths of the pine-scented air and tried to slow his racing heart. He turned his head then, and in the failing light, he saw that it was indeed Llywelyn's elder brother, Owain. Owain smiled at him.

"Sorry about that," he said. "I had to make sure you weren't an English soldier." Olan nodded in understanding.

"Couldn't you tell if I was an English soldier or not?" Olan asked.

"No. The light is too poor to see clearly who it was. I didn't know you were a Welshman until you spoke," Owain said rubbing his hands together.

"You are Lord Owain aren't you?" Owain nodded.

"Yes, I am." He confirmed. "Do you know where my brother is?"

"Yes, he is a short distance away through these trees. I can take you to him if you like?" Olan said reaching out to pick up the kettle. Owain quickly picked up the fish and one of the water skins, leaving Olan to pick up the other. Then they both stood up and Olan led Owain back through the trees towards the clearing.

Llywelyn turned his head at the sound of footsteps and saw in relief that it was Olan back with water. He had been gone a long time and he had begun to worry.

"Olan, there you are," he said a little reproachfully. "What kept you?"

"Sorry about that. I met someone at the stream." Olan said placing the kettle and water skins he was carrying on the ground close to the fire.

"It wasn't an English soldier was it?" Llywelyn asked concerned. Olan shook his head.

"No, it wasn't an English soldier," he said with a grin. He picked up the kettle and placed it on a large rock in the center of the fire to boil. Then picking up a water skin he walked over to the horses and held it open for them to drink.

"Who was it then?" Llywelyn asked curiously. Olan grinned again and took the now empty skin over to where the saddlebags lay under a tree and dropped it down beside them. He stood up then and turned to face the trees.

"Well, why don't you show yourself?" he said. Llywelyn looked at him confused. He was about to open his mouth to speak when Owain detached himself from the shadows and stepped into the firelight.

"It was me," he said.

Llywelyn looked up at him in shock and disbelief from where he sat on the ground. Feeling uncomfortable he stood up to get a good look at his brother. Despite weeks of good food and lots of rest, his face was gaunt, and he could see dark circles under his eyes. His eyes had a hard look to them now that they had never had before. It must have been his years of imprisonment that did it Llywelyn thought. Or maybe it was watching their father die right in front of him. He smiled at his brother.

"Owain, is it really you?" Owain smiled at him in return.

"Yes, it is me. Or what is left of me anyway."

Llywelyn laughed and walking over to his brother embraced him briefly. "It is so good to see you," he said. "What are you doing here though?"

"Our darling uncle has declared war on England," Owain said. "Here, I am guessing you want these." He held out the string of fish and Olan took them smiling his thanks. He stuck each fish on a stick and stabbed the sticks into the soil around the edge of the fire ring to cook. Owain sat down beside the fire to warm himself and Llywelyn sat down beside him.

"I know. I gave him your letter," Llywelyn said stretching his legs out in front of him with a sigh of relaxation.

"I knew you would have no choice but to do so. I just didn't think it would lead to all-out war," Owain said reaching his hands towards the fire to warm them.

"Dafydd has been trying to find a way out of that treaty from the day he signed it," Llywelyn said.

"Why? It favored him in every way," Owain said surprised.

"I have been watching him closely while you have been away, and I have seen more of that man than you have ever have in all your years. You should have seen his face when he read your letter. I don't think I have ever seen anyone so angry before in my life."

"If he didn't want to sign that treaty then why did he?"

"His back was against the wall. He had no choice."

"There is always a choice."

"This is exactly why you could never be a ruler. Your hot head gets in your way too often and so you can't see what is there in front of you." Owain looked at his brother in surprise.

"That's what you think is it?" Llywelyn shook his head.

"That is what I know. I took on the position of head warrior shortly after you and father were taken away and I know things that you will never know," he said.

"Care to share some of them with me?"

"Not right now, no," Owain shrugged.

"I have something for you," he said. He put his hand in the pocket of his cloak and pulled out the written account of his time at Winchester Castle and handed it to his brother.

"What's this?" Llywelyn asked.

"It is a written account of my time at Winchester Castle. Everything I heard and witnessed during my stay there, including the King's war council," Owain said with a note of pride in his voice.

Llywelyn smiled at him and unfolded the roll of parchment and began to read. He read it over quickly and then refolding it placed it in his pocket to go over more thoroughly later.

"This information will be especially useful. Dafydd will be grateful to have it," he said. The smell of roasting fish was strong now and Owain felt his stomach grumble in anticipation. He had stopped having fires once he had gotten close to the border between the two lands so he wouldn't be detected by the wrong people. So he had been surviving on whatever plants and berries he would find along the way and hadn't had a hot meal in several days. Just the thought of the hot flaky fish was making his mouth water.

"You said you have taken over father's position as head warrior?" he said trying to distract himself from the smell of the roasting fish.

"Yes, I have," Llywelyn said. "I took on the job as soon as I found out that you and father had been taken to England."

"Are you enjoying it?"

"Yes, I am. It keeps me busy." Olan cleared his voice to interrupt.

"The food is ready," he said. He pulled out three bowls and being incredibly careful not to burn his hand he began to pull the sticks from the edge of the fire and he placed the fish in the bowls. Then he handed one each to the two brothers before sitting down to eat his own. The fish was flaking and looked so good that Owain had to stop himself from just swallowing them whole. He chewed on each one and forced himself to eat slowly to avoid the little fish bones. The last thing he wanted was to choke to death because he was being too hasty.

"So what happened when my letter reached you?" he asked after a few minutes.

"Well, I read it and so did mother, and then I took it to Dafydd. He took one look at it and then turned to me and said he was declaring war on England. I was given the task of finding Captain Carrol and together we gathered the troops and put them through a few weeks of intense training to prepare them for battle. Then I packed up my things and rode north to scout out the situation with the English army," Llywelyn said spitting out a fishbone. "What about you?"

"I stayed at Winchester Castle as long as I could to gather as much information as possible. But after I overheard the King's war council I knew it was time to leave. I stayed just long enough to write that account and then I stole a horse from the stables and left."

Llywelyn grinned at him. "You stole a horse right from under the King's nose?"

"Yep. How do you think I got here so quickly?"

"Where is it now?" Olan asked.

"The bitch bucked me off a few days back when she heard another horse in the English camp call out. I have been on foot ever since," Owain said picking up his last fish and popping it into his mouth.

"Olan and I are leaving to find the Welsh army in the morning. You are welcome to join us if you like," Llywelyn said as he began tossing his fishbones in the fire. Then he placed his now empty bowl on the ground and wiped his mouth with the back of his hand.

"I would thank you," Owain said beginning to toss his fishbones in the fire.

"Great. You can double with Olan until we can find you a horse. I am sure they will have a spare mount in the Welsh camp."

Owain nodded.

Llywelyn stretched and gave a wide yawn. "We should get some sleep. There is a spare blanket in the saddlebags you can use," he said pointing.

"Thanks," Owain said. He stood up and walking over to the saddlebags pulled out the spare blanket. Then he walked back to the fire. They all rolled themselves in their blankets then and went to sleep by the fire.

The next morning, they woke to the sound of birds chirping in the trees and began to strike camp. The fire had gone out in the night. Llywelyn gathered up the rocks that had made up the fire ring and tossed them haphazardly into the trees. Then he scattered the ashes from the fire. They didn't want to leave any sign that they had camped there.

Owain helped Olan ready the horses while Llywelyn erased the signs of the fire. Then they finished by buckling on the saddlebags and Llywelyn's sword onto the saddles before mounting up. Owain mounted up behind Olan. Then with one last look at the clearing, they gave the horses a light kick and rode back towards the road to go and find the Welsh army.

Chapter 14

An Unexpected Meeting

They finally reached the Welsh army after about a week of searching. A Welsh sentry saw them coming and waved them to a halt.

"State your name and purpose," the man said in a commanding voice. Llywelyn smiled at the man.

"I am Llywelyn ap Gruffudd. Nephew to the Prince and head warrior," he said. The man bowed his head in shame.

"I am so sorry, My Lord. I did not recognize you at first," he said.

"It is all right. You were just doing your job," Llywelyn said and pointed to Olan and Owain. "They are with me." The man nodded his head.

"Yes, of course," he said and stood aside to let them pass.

As they rode through the camp there seemed to be a constant sense of movement. Some men sharpened weapons, while others looked after the animals. Then others were either eating or playing at cards or dice around small individual campfires.

Owain stared in wonderment as they rode. It seemed that every able-bodied man had come to fight for the cause. There was a constant hum of talk and a palpable buzz of excitement among the men. For some of the younger men, this would be their first time on the battlefield. He guessed that they were still under the illusion of the glory it would bring them. He had felt the same way at their age. That was until he had fought a few battles and realized that there was no glory in it at all. He wished that he were still that young and naive man again riding off to his first battle with not a care in the world. Life was so much simpler then. His father had still alive then and so had his grandfather. Two people that had meant the world to him, and now they were both gone forever, and he knew too well what happened in war.

"I think I see it," Olan said a few minutes later.

"See what?" Llywelyn asked.

"The command tent," Olan replied.

"Where?" Owain asked.

"Over there," Olan said pointing. They both looked where Olan was pointing and saw it as well. It stood much taller among the slightly smaller ones that surrounded it.

"Olan, why don't you take the horses and find us a place to camp. Preferably in the woods somewhere away from the rest of the encampment and Owain and I will go and pay Dafydd a visit," Llywelyn said as he pulled his horse to a halt.

Olan nodded. "All right," he said. Llywelyn and Owain dismounted and Olan took Arling's reins in one hand. Then he rode away to find them a place to camp.

Owain shrugged and turned to his brother. "Well let's get going then," he said in a flat voice. He was not looking forward to this meeting. Llywelyn nodded in agreement and they started to walk through the camp in the direction of the command tent.

They reached the ring of guards surrounding the command tent a few minutes later and stopped. Llywelyn squared his shoulders and cleared his throat to speak.

"I am Llywelyn ap Gruffudd, nephew to the Prince and head warrior," he said in his most commanding voice. "I am here to give my report. The guards all nodded in recognition and stood aside. Llywelyn nodded in thanks and he and Owain walked through into the tent.

Dafydd was sitting at a table in the center of the tent poring over some papers when they entered. In one corner, there was a battered chest, and in the other a small sleeping cot. Just the sight of the man made Owain's blood boil. He walked over to the table and stood looming over him.

"Hello Dafydd," Owain said quietly. Dafydd jumped and dropped the paper he was holding. He looked up and was given a shock to see the change in Owain. His face was almost unrecognizable, and his eyes had a hard quality that they had never had before. Dafydd swallowed and cleared his throat.

"Owain, it is good to see you. How are you?" he said in a shaky voice.

Owain glared at him. "How do you think I am?" he snapped. "My father is dead."

"I am so sorry about that. It was a shock for all of us," Dafydd said attempting to console.

"You are sorry?" Owain said, his voice breaking on the sorry. "He is dead because of you."

"My hands were tied," Dafydd said attempting to justify his actions.

"Save me your lies. They won't work with me."

"What do you want from me? Don't you think I would have done something more to get you both out of there long before now? I had no choice but to do what I did. I'm sorry," Dafydd said getting angry himself now.

"You always have a choice," Owain said reminding himself eerily of his father just before he fell to his death.

Dafydd glared at his nephew in turn. "Be careful what you say. I am your Prince," he said.

"No, you are not," Owain retorted. "The only reason I came back from England was to help Llywelyn. As far as I am concerned, you could die tomorrow, and I would not shed a single tear."

"Get out," Dafydd growled.

"Gladly," Owain said and giving his uncle one last scathing look turned and left the tent, and walking right past Llywelyn without a single glance. Dafydd shook his head. He doubted that he would ever be able to make Owain understand the guilt he felt for his brother's death. Everything he had told him was true, but it didn't change how he felt about it all.

Llywelyn detached himself from the shadows by the tent flap and walked over to the table. Dafydd turned his head and seeing who it was sighed in relief. He motioned for him to sit, and pulling out a chair, Llywelyn sat down opposite his uncle.

"Have you come to yell at me as well?" Dafydd asked. Llywelyn shook his head.

"No," he said quietly.

Dafydd gave him a smile of appreciation. "Thank you," he said.

Llywelyn nodded his head. "I have come to give you my report," he said. Dafydd perked up at this.

"Oh, good. What have you found?" he asked excitedly. Llywelyn smiled and pulled Owain's account from his pocket and slid it across the table to him.

"You might want to read that," he said.

"What is it?"

"A written account of everything Owain heard and witnessed while he was at the King's court, including the war council, he overheard just before he left," Llywelyn explained.

Dafydd opened the scroll of parchment and began to read.

Llywelyn sat in silence while he watched his uncle reading his brother's account. He had read it over at least three times himself during the week that it took to find the Welsh army camp, and so he knew everything that it said. He thought about his brother and what he must be feeling. He understood both sides. He knew how hard it had been for Dafydd to do what he had done. But he could also imagine just how it must have been for Owain locked away for four years in that cold stone tower with little food and their depressed father as company. Owain had explained to him the mental state of Gruffudd before his death, and it had sounded like his spirit had broken.

"Thank you for bringing this to me," Dafydd said a few minutes later as he placed the account back on the table.

"I thought you would find it interesting. At least you know now that Owain hasn't just been sitting around doing nothing for the past few months while he has been recovering at the King's court," Llywelyn said. Dafydd nodded.

"I can see that," he said. "When you see him, tell him I am sorry. I know he won't believe it, but it is true. I am sorry."

Llywelyn smiled at him. "I know you are," he said. Dafydd smiled back and cleared his throat.

"How about some brandy?" he said standing up.

"That would be nice thank you," Dafydd walked over to the chest in the corner and opening it pulled out two cups. Then he walked back to the table and sat down. He poured brandy into each of the cups from the decanter that sat on the table and handed one to Llywelyn. He took it with a nod of thanks and took a sip.

"So, what can you tell me of the English army?" Dafydd asked taking a sip from his cup.

"It took me a little while to find them, but I caught up with them eventually," Llywelyn said taking another sip of brandy. "It looks like they crossed into Gwynedd about two weeks ago or so, but I can't be entirely sure. I have only seen foot soldiers though, no cavalry."

"From what Owain says in his report the King plans to send his cavalry on after the foot soldiers," Dafydd said.

"Yes, and from what I have seen it seems he is doing exactly that. Cavalry can move faster than foot soldiers, so I imagine they will cross the border fairly soon."

"How long do you think before they reach us?"

"Maybe a month? I can't be sure," Dafydd nodded.

"Well, I don't want you to scout for me anymore. I will send someone else to do that. I rather have you working with Carrol to drill the men."

"Of course," Llywelyn said taking another sip. "What about Owain?"

"What about him?" Dafydd said taking a sip from his cup.

"What do you want to do with him?"

"I am not going to punish him for speaking his mind."

"Oh, good," Llywelyn said in relief.

"See if he will help you and Carrol with the men. It will give him something to do," Dafydd suggested. Llywelyn nodded.

"Good idea," he said and drained his cup. Then he stood up to leave. "I need to go and find out where Olan has got to. I sent him to find us a place to camp," Dafydd nodded in understanding.

"Of course. Come here in the morning and we can go over things with Carrol and some of the other officers," he said.

"I will be here."

"Bring Owain as well if you can."

"I will try," Llywelyn said with a smile. Then he turned and left the tent to find his brother.

Dafydd finished his drink alone with his thoughts. He thought about everything that had happened and what it all meant. The sight of Owain's gaunt face and hard cold eyes haunted him. What had happened to him to make him so hard? He doubted he would ever tell him the truth. Maybe it was the years of imprisonment that had done it? On the other hand, it could have been the shock of seeing his father die right in front of him. All he knew is that he no longer knew the man. He hoped that Llywelyn would be able to work with him and help him to control his anger enough to be a useful soldier in the upcoming battle. The last thing he needed was for Owain to lose his head on the battlefield and jeopardize them all. He trusted that Llywelyn would do his best. But would it be enough he wondered? He didn't know.

He poured himself a second cup of brandy and took a long swallow. He picked up Owain's written account and read it through again while he continued to drink. Everything he had written was especially useful and he wanted to memorize the account by heart. He didn't think it would be safe to keep it around and wanted to get rid of it as soon as possible so it didn't fall into the wrong hands. It was just his sense of caution talking, but it hadn't done him wrong thus far. So he would memorize it and then burn it the first chance he had. He couldn't be sure they didn't have at least one spy in the camp, so he wasn't going to take any chances.

Chapter 15

The Front Lines

Llywelyn found his brother a short distance away from the tent staring at the organized chaos of the Welsh encampment.

Owain turned at his step and sighed with relief to see him."I was wondering when you would be finished," he said.

"Are you all right?" Llywelyn asked concerned.

"No," Owain admitted. "I never should have gone to see him. It just brought it all back."

"What do you mean?"

"Everything. The years of imprisonment, father's death, everything."

Llywelyn placed a comforting hand on his brother's shoulder. "I know this probably won't mean anything to you, but Dafydd wanted you to know he is truly sorry."

Owain barked laughter.

"You are right, that means nothing to me," he said.

Llywelyn gave his shoulder a quick squeeze and then let go. "Come on, let's go and find Olan and see if he has managed to make something to eat. I'm starving."

Owain nodded in agreement and they began to walk through the encampment together.

The camp just seemed to get bigger and bigger the farther they walked. The combination of unwashed bodies, campfire smoke, and animals was so pervasive it was like a slap in the face after the smells of the forest. They both longed to find Olan and some fresher air. But the camp seemed endless.

"Where do you think he is?" Owain asked after some time had passed.

Llywelyn shook his head. "Your guess is as good as mine," he said. "Somewhere away from all of this I hope," Owain nodded.

"Do you think they ever sleep?"

"I don't know," Llywelyn said. "I suppose some of the men do. But there will always be someone awake at all hours of the day and night. You remember battle camps, don't you?"

Owain shook his head. "Not really. It has been so long since I have seen a battlefield," he said.

"True enough," Llywelyn agreed.

"Lucky for Dafydd that he has that tent. It must block out some of this noise."

"Yes," Llywelyn agreed.

After what felt like an eternity, they came to the edge of the woods. Sighing in relief, they stepped into the trees. The moment they entered the woods silence fell around them and they both took deep breaths of the crisp pine-scented air. Then they began to move through the trees in search of Olan and the horses.

Dead leaves crunched underfoot as they made their way through the woods as they searched.

"How can anyone breathe in let alone sleep in that camp?" Owain said reveling in the fresh clean air of the woods.

Llywelyn shook his head. "I have no idea," he said.

The light was beginning to fade and cast shadows amongst the branches. Llywelyn was beginning to be concerned that they would have to make their own camp for the night and try to find Olan in the morning when they finally found him. They saw firelight peeking out from between two oak trees and made their way towards it. Then as they stepped through the trees they found themselves in a small clearing with a blazing fire in the middle of it. Olan was standing beside the fire and stirring something in the large iron kettle. He turned his head at the sound of their footsteps and smiled to see them.

"There you two are," he said. "I was beginning to wonder if you had gotten lost or something."

"We nearly did," Llywelyn said walking over to where the water skins sat on the ground under one of the trees. He picked up one, and opening it drank deeply.

"That smells delicious Olan," Owain said, his mouth beginning to water.

"Thank you. It is nearly ready," Olan said with a smile of appreciation.

Owain walked over to the fire and reached his hands out towards the heat to warm them. Llywelyn finished drinking and lay the water skin back on the ground where he had found it. Then he walked over to join the other two by the fire. Olan tested the contents of the kettle and found it was ready. He leaned down and picked up their wooden bowls he had pulled out of the saddlebags and began spooning stew into them. Then he handed one each to Llywelyn and Owain before filling a third for himself.

The darkness in the woods was complete, and the only source of light was the fire burning brightly in the middle of the clearing. It didn't bother Llywelyn in the slightest though. Years of scouting and traveling through the land of Gwynedd as head warrior had made him used to the silence and the complete darkness of the woods. Quite often he would choose to sleep in the woods rather than at an inn or someone's house with people he didn't know.

Starving the two brothers sat down to eat the dark rich stew.

"Is this venison?" Owain asked. Olan nodded his head.

"Yes, it is. One of the soldiers shot a deer and gave me enough for a stew. I thought it would make a nice change from dried meat," he said raising another spoonful of stew to his mouth.

"Yes, it is a nice change. Thank you, Olan." Llywelyn said scooping up another spoonful. Owain nodded his head in agreement being unable to speak with a mouth full of hot stew.

"Oh, I forgot to ask, how did it go with the Prince? Did you manage to give him your report?" Olan asked. Llywelyn nodded.

"Yes, I gave him my report and he read over the account that you wrote Owain. He was incredibly pleased to have it," he said. Owain gave a non-committal grunt.

"That is good," Olan said putting another spoonful of stew into his mouth.

"Dafydd wants your help Owain," Llywelyn said looking at his brother.

"Help with what?"

"He wants you to be a part of the battle plans along with myself and Carrol."

Owain shook his head. "Why does he want my help if he already has you and Carrol?"

"Because you are a very good strategist, and also to give you something to do."

"I see." Llywelyn scraped the bottom of his bowl with his spoon to get the last of the stew.

"He is having a meeting at his tent in the morning with Carrol and the rest of the commanding officers and he wants us both to be there."

"Do I have to go?"

"No, but I think you should," Llywelyn said placing his empty bowl on the ground.

"I will think about it," Owain said. Llywelyn nodded his head in acquiescence. He couldn't expect much more than that from him he thought. So he didn't push the subject.

A short distance away the horses stood hobbled and eating the last remains of grass growing under the trees. A third horse beside them happily cropping at the grass beneath the trees. She was a tall dark brown horse with a black mane and tail and wide shoulders.

Owain noticed the unfamiliar horse and pointed to her. "Whose horse is that?" he asked.

"She is yours," Olan said scraping the bottom of his bowl with his spoon for any remaining pieces of meat. "Really? Where did you get her?" Owain asked. Olan put down his empty bowl and wiped his mouth with the back of his hand.

"I saw her standing alone in a rope paddock and asked if she belonged to anyone. Apparently, she was brought along as a spare mount. I asked if I could take her and they agreed. I figured you would need a horse of your own come the fighting."

Owain shook his head in surprise."Thank you, Olan. That was very thoughtful. What is her name?"

"River," Olan said pouring a small amount of water into his bowl to rinse it. Owain and Llywelyn did the same and then packed the bowls away in one of the saddlebags.

Owain walked over to the horses and placed his hand on River's shoulder.

"Hello there," he said stroking his hand down her side. She raised her head momentarily and blew softly in his face. Then she resumed cropping at the grass. He took an overall view of her and smiled. She was more than capable of carrying him into battle. He gave her one last pat and then walked back to the fire.

"What do you think of her?" Olan asked as he sat back down.

"She is a good-looking horse. Very sturdy. I think she will do nicely."

Olan smiled with pleasure knowing that he had been able to help Owain in this small way.

As Llywelyn drifted off to sleep he thought about his brother. Something had changed in him and he wondered if he would ever be the same person he had known before ever again. He worried that he would do something to their uncle in his rage. Owain had always been hot-headed, even as a small child. But what he had witnessed when he met Dafydd again for the first time since his imprisonment four years previously was something else entirely. The look on his face as he had raged at the man made him look like a total stranger and it had scared Llywelyn to no end. Maybe Dafydd was right. Maybe giving Owain a job to do would help. He hoped it would.

The next morning during breakfast Owain turned to his brother.

"I have made my decision," he said spooning the last of his porridge into his mouth and swallowing.

"Oh?" Owain wiped his mouth with the back of his hand and placed his empty bowl on the ground. "I will come with you to see Dafydd today, and I will help our soldiers to victory," he said.

Llywelyn smiled at his brother.

"Thank you," he said. He felt more than a little relieved to hear it. He hadn't been lying when he had said that Owain was a good strategist, and the Welsh army would benefit from his guidance. With his expertise, they might just have a chance of winning this war.

After breakfast, they mounted up and rode out of the clearing in the direction of the command tent. It was a much faster trip through the camp on horseback than it had been the night before on foot. The camp looked much different in the daylight, a little more friendly and inviting than it had in the semi-darkness of the previous evening. The noise level hadn't changed though and there was still that sense of controlled chaos about the place.

Once they reached the tent they dismounted and left their horses in the hands of the guards. Then they walked together into the tent. The army captain Carol was already seated at the table in the middle of the tent along with some of the other high-ranking officers. Dafydd saw them and waved them over. The two brothers walked to the table and sat down on either side of the Prince.

"Llywelyn, Owain, thank you for coming this morning," he said with a smile.

"Sorry, we are late," Llywelyn said apologetically.

"You are here now, and that is all that matters," Dafydd said kindly.

"I am telling you it won't work," Carrol said continuing an argument he and Dafydd had been having before Llywelyn and Owain had arrived.

"Are you questioning your Prince?"

Carrol shook his head. "No, I am simply stating the facts. A battle is never won defensively."

"He is right you know." Llywelyn chimed in. Owain nodded in agreement.

"Yes, he is," he said.

"I see," Dafydd said. Carrol glared at him.

"You will take their word but not mine?" he said defensively.

Dafydd shook his head. "No, I am not taking sides. Now that you have all explained this to me I have no choice but to accept it is true," he said. "Besides Owain was always one of the best strategists in the land, and Llywelyn is my head warrior."

Carrol sneered. "Owain has been living at Winchester Castle in England for the past several months since his release from prison. Who's to say he isn't the King's spy."

"Because he brought me this," Dafydd said sliding Owain's written account across the table to him.

"What's this?" Carrol asked.

"A written account of everything Owain heard and witnessed in his time at the King's court," Dafydd said. "Go ahead and read it for yourself." Carrol picked it up and began to read. He reached the bottom of the page and laid it back on the table. Then he turned his head to look at Owain.

"Is this all true?" he asked.

"Yes, every word," Owain replied.

He bowed his head in shame. "I'm sorry. Maybe you aren't working for the King after all," he said in apology.

"No, I am not," Owain confirmed.

"I'm sorry for misjudging you."

Owain shook his head."Don't worry about it. You are right; I have been at the King's court for several months. So you had every right to suspect me of being a spy. But I assure you I am not one," he said.

Carrol nodded. "Yes, I see that now," he said and turned his attention to Llywelyn.

"What do you think we should do?"

"We need to strike first and make them afraid of us. From the little of their army that I have seen so far, they are more than a match for us."

Owain nodded in agreement. “The King is sending his entire force to meet us, and it is considerable. My brother has only seen the contingent of foot soldiers so far. But I am sure they will be sending the cavalry on shortly to join them.” The men around the table shuttered at the news of such a force.

“We still need to drill the men hard, so they are more than ready to meet the English,” Llywelyn said. “From what I saw it looks like we have at least a month before they reach us, maybe six weeks.” The men all nodded in understanding.

“I want the three of you to work together in this,” Dafydd said pointing to first Carrol and then to Owain and Llywelyn. They all nodded.

“I would love to have both of your thoughts on battle tactics,” Carrol said. The two brothers nodded in agreement.

“Good,” Dafydd said with a smile. “I think that concludes this meeting.” Everyone stood up then and began to file out of the tent.

Carrol walked beside the two brothers to retrieve his horse from the guards. “How about we meet tomorrow for lunch to go over things,” he suggested.

“We are camped in the woods,” Llywelyn said. “Why don’t you come to our camp and we can discuss things there. It is much quieter than this.” Carrol nodded.

“Where in the woods?” he asked.

“Not far. Once you enter the trees turn left and within a short distance you will see our fire,” Owain explained.

“All right I will come to your camp for lunch tomorrow,” Carrol agreed.

They all mounted up then and rode away in different directions. Owain and Llywelyn rode in the direction of their camp in the woods and Carrol deeper into the main encampment. They returned to find Olan cooking something on the fire. It smelled delicious and Llywelyn felt his stomach growl with hunger.

"So how did it go?" Olan asked.

"Carrol and Dafydd were arguing about how best to fight a battle," Llywelyn said sitting down by the fire. He stretched out his legs and sighed with pleasure. "It took myself and Owain to finally convince him that a battle is never won defensively."

Olan shook his head in confusion. "I thought that was common knowledge?" he said.

"Apparently not," Llywelyn said with a shrug.

"The man's an idiot," Owain said sitting down next to his brother.

"He is just uneducated about battle tactics," Llywelyn said in their uncle's defense. "He didn't spend a lot of time on the battlefield as father did."

"Why do you keep defending him?" Owain asked.

"Because he has an exceedingly difficult job and is only trying to do his best for his people. It is a job I certainly would never want, and I admire him for taking it on." Llywelyn said picking up a water skin and taking a long drink.

"If you say so," Owain said taking the water skin that Llywelyn offered him.

"Food's ready," Olan announced.

"Great, I'm starved," Llywelyn said. Olan spooned soup into two bowls and passed one each to the two brothers. Then he filled a third for himself and they all sat down to eat.

The next day Carrol came to find them in their camp in the woods. Hearing the sound of another horse all three of their horses called out in greeting to the newcomer. Carol's horse called back as he rode into the clearing.

"You found it," Llywelyn said with a smile. Carrol nodded and dismounted. He hobbled his horse next to the others and walked over to where the two brothers sat by the fire.

"It wasn't hard to find really," he said sitting down. "You are right though. It is much quieter here in the woods."

"That is why I suggested it," Llywelyn said.

"Tea sir?" Olan asked holding out a steaming cup to Carrol. He nodded and took the cup gratefully.

"Thank you," he said and took a careful sip of the hot tea.

"Well, shall we get down to business?" Llywelyn said accepting his cup of tea with a nod of thanks.

"Sure." Carrol agreed.

They spent the next few hours discussing different battle tactics. Carrol asked Owain all about the King and what he knew of the English army.

"The King won't be leading them," Owain said accepting a bowl of hot soup from Olan with a nod of thanks. Olan handed one to both Llywelyn and Carrol in turn before filling one for himself.

"It will be his son right?" Carrol said dipping a spoon into his bowl.

"Yes," Owain confirmed.

"What do you think of him?"

"I only saw him a few times during my stay. But he is incredibly young," Owain said putting another spoonful of soup into his mouth.

"He is the same age as I am," Llywelyn said. Owain nodded.

"Yes, but you look older and are much more mature than he is."

"His inexperience might be to our advantage," Carrol said dipping his spoon back into his bowl for another spoonful of soup.

"Very true," Llywelyn agreed.

"He will have the King's best knight and the army general to help him though." Owain reminded them.

"True," Llywelyn said.

After they had talked for a long time Carrol stood up to leave.

"Well I think we have a plan," he said walking over to his horse.

"Yes, I think so." Llywelyn agreed. "Owain and I will meet you in the morning to start drilling the men."

"I will see you both then. Thank you for lunch." He mounted up and rode out of the clearing. Owain watched him go.

"He knows his stuff. It is good Dafydd has him to lead the army," he said.

Llywelyn nodded. "Father always spoke well of the man."

"I can see why," Owain said.

"We need more water. I will go and get some more," Llywelyn said. He picked up the water skins and walked into the trees to find water.

For the next several weeks, Llywelyn along with Carrol and his brother Owain drilled the men with the help of the other officers. Each night the two brothers returned to their camp in the woods exhausted. They would eat a quick supper and then roll themselves in their blankets by the fire and fall fast asleep. It felt good to be doing something productive for a change.

It had been so long since he had trained, and he found that his strength was not what it had been. So Owain worked twice as hard as the rest of the men to build up his strength so he would be ready for the upcoming battle. Holding a sword in his hand once more made him feel like he was regaining a part of himself that he had lost years before. As he practiced sword fighting with the men or the art of shooting a longbow he felt that he was truly home.

Chapter 16

Blades and Bandages

About six weeks later, Llywelyn came awake with the feeling that something had happened. Something important and he didn't know what. In their clearing, they were cut off from the main camp and so they couldn't hear anything that might be going on.

He turned his head and saw that his brother was also awake.

"Good morning," Owain said. Llywelyn nodded in reply.

"Can you hear anything?" he asked. Owain shook his head.

"No, why?"

"I thought I heard something," Llywelyn replied. He shrugged and stood up. "I must have imagined it." He turned then and walked into the trees to relieve himself.

When he returned, he found Olan preparing breakfast. A few minutes later, they had all sat down to eat when there came the sound of horse hooves. Their three horses heard the sound and called out in greeting. Llywelyn and

Owain put down their bowls and stood up just as the lone rider entered the clearing.

"My Lords, the Prince requests your presence right away," the servant named Huw said slightly out of breath.

"What has happened?" Llywelyn asked.

"A scout came a short time ago to tell the Prince that he saw the English army and they are almost here."

"Tell my uncle that we will be with him shortly."

Huw nodded his head and giving his horse a light kick rode back the way he had come.

After Huw had gone, the three men flew into action. Llywelyn and Owain pulled on their armor while Olan saddled the horses. They picked up their weapons and buckled them onto their saddles. Llywelyn turned to his friend.

"Where will you be?" he asked.

"I thought I would go to the hospital tents and try to make myself useful there," Olan replied.

"That sounds like a good idea. You should be safe enough there." Olan nodded.

The two brothers mounted up then and rode out of the clearing to join the rest of the Welsh army.

Olan packed away the rest of the camp supplies and hung the saddlebags from a low-hanging tree branch in case any wild animals came looking for food. Then he put out the fire and tried not to let himself worry about his friend. But it wasn't easy.

He saddled his horse Joh and mounting up rode out of the clearing to find the hospital tents. He figured that would be a good place to be during a battle. He would have plenty to keep him occupied which would help to keep him from worrying, and he would be kept informed of what was going on at the same time.

He found the hospital tents fairly quickly. They were just outside the main camp close to the edge of the trees. When he reached the tents he dismounted and waited for someone to show themselves. He didn't want to just barge in and frighten anyone. So he stood there holding Joh's reins in one hand and waited.

He didn't have to wait long, however. A few minutes after he arrived, a short man with medium-length brown hair and round deep green eyes saw him standing there and walked up to him. Olan could see that he wore a long coat with rust spots around the sleeves which he suddenly realized must be dried blood. He shuttered inwardly at the thought.

"Can I help you?" the man asked. He had a surprisingly deep voice for such a small man. Olan nodded his head.

"I have come to see if I could be of any help to you here," he said.

"What's your name?" the man asked.

"My name is Olan. I am Lord Llywelyn's man-servant."

The man nodded in understanding. "Can you set bones at all?"

Olan smiled and nodded. "I can do that. I can also stitch minor wounds and tie a good bandage. When you serve a warrior you learn how to do such things," he said. The man smiled back at him.

"It must be a hard job." Olan shook his head.

"Not at all. It is an honor to do it."

"I would very much appreciate the help. You can tie your horse to the wagon there next to mine. There is a barrel full of linens that you can start tearing into bandages when you are done. I have a feeling we are going to need quite a lot before too long. Battles are always such bloody affairs." Olan nodded and tied Joh to the wagon that stood a short distance away.

"Oh, you didn't tell me your name," he said.

"My name is Roland."

"It is nice to meet you, Roland," Olan said with a smile. He walked over to the large barrel he could see full of linens and sat down on the ground beside it. Then he began to tear different lengths of bandages.

The moment Llywelyn and Owain entered the Welsh camp; they found it a hive of activity. Men rushed about gathering weapons and saddling horses while officers yelled instructions.

The two brothers rode through the camp in search of Dafydd and Captain Carrol. Men stared as they rode by in their battle armor. They must have looked impressive for some of the younger men gazed at them with admiration. Most of the men had only leather-plated armor, while others had nothing at all. It was only the officers that had chainmail or plate armor. Being royal and therefore extremely high ranking indeed both brothers war plate armor with the family insignia stamped into the chest plates.

They found the Prince and the captain after about 20 minutes or so of searching. Dafydd saw them and waved to them. He looked relieved to see them. Carrol smiled at them as they rode up to them.

"There you two are. I was beginning to worry," Dafydd said.

"Sorry, it took some time to get here," Llywelyn said apologetically. "Are they here yet?"

Dafydd shook his head. "Not yet. But I am sure they will be here any minute," he said. They all fell silent then and waited for the English army to come.

Llywelyn sat on his horse next to Owain and thought about all the battles he had fought in. Every bone in his body was on fire with adrenalin. He would never admit it to anyone, but there was something about the fight that made him feel alive in a way that nothing else ever had. That being said he had never been in love and he imagined that this must be what it felt like in bed with a woman that you loved. He was just guessing though.

He mentally shook himself and tried to turn off all his emotions. It wouldn't do to think about what he was about to do. It would mess with his concentration and make him vulnerable. So he breathed deeply and tried to think about nothing at all, letting his mind drift as he listened to the sounds of the men around him, as they prepared for the fight to come.

It felt like a long time before the call came from the scout that the English were coming. He came galloping up to Dafydd and skidded to a halt just before he reached them.

"They are here. The English are here," he said panting.

"How close?" Dafydd demanded, but there was no need to ask. There came the sound of battle horns and Llywelyn could see the foot soldiers marching in formation towards them. Carrol looked to Dafydd.

"It is your call," he said. Dafydd nodded and swallowed. Just for a second Llywelyn thought he saw something like fear cross his uncle's face, but it was gone in seconds. He raised his sword high for all to see and his voice rang out across the battlefield.

"Charge!"

As Llywelyn rode into the battle, he was pleased to find his mind was clear of all thought. He acted on instinct as he rode at full speed into the fray. His horse Arling carried him through the scores of soldiers with ease. He had trained her for war, and she hadn't let him down yet.

The fighting became intense and ferocious within minutes with neither side giving quarter. All he could hear was the sound of clashing swords and the screaming of both horses and men. The world had turned red with blood and the ground was soon slippery with it as well as other more unpleasant substances. Those men that fell were trampled by both horses and soldiers alike.

From time to time, he caught glances of his brother riding at full speed and using his bow to devastating effect. Of the two of them, Owain had always been the better archer. He narrowly missed being hit by an arrow himself fired from a foot soldier. He leaned down from the saddle and with a quick swipe of his sword cut the man down without ceremony. Then he sat upright again and kept moving. All the while keeping his eyes peeled for possible threats or targets.

Each time a man was brought to the hospital tents to be tended, Olan would check his face to assure himself that it wasn't Llywelyn. He was not only his lord, but also his friend and he didn't know what he would do if he died. He understood that it was a risk that came with the job of a warrior. But so far he had managed to keep his friend safe from harm. But he couldn't be out there on the battlefield with him watching his back and it ate at him.

Over the course of the day, he found himself setting bones and tying a lot of bandages. Sometimes if a wound was too great to mend he would simply hold the man's hand and try to give him some comfort as he died. It wasn't much, but at least they didn't die alone.

As the light began to fade, Olan put down the length of cloth he had been attempting to tear in two for a couple more bandages and stood up. He hadn't realized how late it was. He walked over to where Roland was mending a man's shoulder to tell him he would need to leave to get back to their camp in the woods before Llywelyn and Owain. Roland heard his footsteps and looked up.

"I need to get back. I am sure the fighting will be over soon, and I am sure Llywelyn will be tired and starving," he said. Roland nodded in understanding.

"Of course. Thank you for all your help today," he said. Olan smiled at him.

"It was my pleasure. It was nice to be useful. I will come again tomorrow if you wish?"

"That would be great. See you then. Olan nodded and walked over to retrieve his horse. He untied him and mounting up rode off towards the camp in the woods.

As the light began to fade, it became harder to see. It soon became evident that with the growing darkness there was no way to continue the fighting. Each side recalled their troops and the fighting was called off for the day. Each side retreated to their respective camps. Llywelyn looked at the carnage that littered the battlefield. In the growing darkness, it was almost impossible to distinguish who was who among the dead. In the dim light, they all looked the same to him. Seeing the dead lay out on the ground like this, he began to wonder what they were doing here. It all seemed so ridiculous somehow now that the adrenalin was gone, and he was back in his thinking mind. He shook his head.

"Come on," Owain said kindly seeing the look on his brother's face. "Don't think about it too much. It will put off your appetite."

Llywelyn nodded and followed his brother as they rode back in the direction of their camp in the woods.

When they reached their camp in the woods, they found the fire already blazing. Olan stood by the fire stirring something in the big kettle. He turned his head at the sound of their approach and dropped the spoon in the kettle. He walked over to them and took the horses' reins as they dismounted. He quickly unsaddled the horses and hobbled them alongside his horse and left them to crop what grass they could find under the trees. Then he walked back over to the fire and continued to stir the stew.

Llywelyn pulled off his armor and laid it down next to the saddlebags under the trees. Then he picked up one of the water skins and took a long drink from it. Owain pulled off his armor and took the water skin from his brother with a nod of thanks. Llywelyn walked over to the fire and stretched out his hands towards the flames to warm them. He felt exhausted. Every bone in his body ached with fatigue. He sat down on the ground and closed his eyes. He wanted nothing more at that moment than to lay down next to the fire and go to sleep for at least a week. But he knew that wasn't an option.

"How did it go?" Olan asked as he stirred the stew. Llywelyn opened his eyes and shook his head to clear it.

"It is hard to say really," he said. "Neither side would give quarter. If the darkness hadn't come, I think we would probably still be out there fighting."

Owain shook his head. "Oh, I don't know about that," he said walking over and sitting down next to his brother. "I think we were doing rather well."

"If you say so," Llywelyn said stifling a yawn.

"And how was your day?" Owain asked turning his attention to Olan.

"It was interesting," he said.

"Really, what happened?" Llywelyn asked.

"I got to set some bones and tie a lot of bandages. The men with the more extensive wounds I left for Roland to take care of. But the conversations between the men who were still able to speak were pretty interesting to listen to." Olan said spooning the stew into two bowls and handing one each to the two brothers. Then he filled a third and sat down to eat his own.

"Who's Roland?" Llywelyn asked blowing on a spoonful of stew before putting it into his mouth.

"He is the army surgeon. He is nice enough. A bit quiet though. Nothing like you two." Owain and Llywelyn laughed at that.

"Oh, yes we are a regular couple of raucous troublemakers," Owain said still laughing. Olan grinned and continued to eat his stew. Owain was finding that each time he smiled it became easier to do it again. It felt good to have banter like this. It reminded him of old times with his family before his father had died and his whole world had changed overnight. It felt like yet another step back to the person he used to be before he had gone to England.

After they finished eating they all rolled themselves in their blankets by the fire and tried to get some sleep before the next day when it would start all over again. Llywelyn lay awake thinking about just how happy he was to hear his brother laughing and making jokes again. He felt like he was slowly beginning to see the person he had known starting to peek out of the shell of the hardened somber man he had become during his years in prison. He hoped for Owain's sake that he continued to try and bring that other person back so he could start to heal. With that thought, he closed his eyes and drifted off to sleep.

Chapter 17

The Taste of Victory

The Welsh and the English battled for several days with neither side giving quarter. Each morning, Olan would see the brothers off and then go to the hospital tents to help Roland with the wounded. All the time while he worked, he prayed that he wouldn't see Llywelyn there among the wounded. It felt to him like the whole world had gone mad. He just wanted it to be over so they could all go home again. He missed Talia and wondered how she was doing. He knew that Llywelyn missed his mother and his two younger brothers and hoped that they would be able to see them all again soon.

One day while he was sitting by the hospital tent tearing some new bandages, a young soldier was brought in for treatment. It was clear right away he was beyond medical help. So he was laid out of the way under a tree while he slowly died from his wounds.

Roland left the man and walked over to where Olan sat. "There is a young man who just came in who is beyond help. Can you go and sit with him?"

Olan nodded and stood up. “Yes, of course,” he said and walked over to where the man lay under the tree. He sat down next to the man and gave him a small smile. He went to pick up his hand when he caught sight of the man’s face and gave a little jump of surprise. The man saw his surprise and smiled weakly at him.

“Hello, Olan, long time no see,” he said in a quiet voice that wouldn’t carry to the rest of the soldiers who were there to be tended.

“Yes, it has been a long time. What are you doing here Arian? The last time I saw you was at the orphanage just before Lord Gruffudd came to take me away to Aberfraw Castle.”

Arian gave a slight nod. “I know. I was adopted a short time after you left by a couple who lived in the village on the outskirts of town there,” Arian explained.

“I see.”

“After a few years though, my father died in an accident, and so it was just myself and my mother left to run the farm for a few years until she died from a cold last winter.”

“I am sorry to hear about your parents,” Olan said squeezing his hand, “So, what are you doing here then?”

“Well after my mother died I didn’t know what to do. I moved into the town and worked at the local inn for a while and then when I heard that they were recruiting people for a war between our land and England, I jumped on the opportunity. I mean it isn’t like I had anything left to live for and I wanted to help if I could.”

Olan nodded in understanding. “I know what you mean. That is why I’m here helping Roland. It is better than sitting back at camp worrying. At least here I can be useful, and I get regular updates on what is going on in the battle against the English from the soldiers who are still able to speak."

"Well, I am happy you are here. I have always wanted to apologize for the way I treated you back in the orphanage."

Olan shook his head at him. "Don't worry about that. It was a long time ago and I am over it now," he said.

"I am still sorry," Arian said and gave Olan's hand a hard squeeze. Then his breathing became labored and when he coughed blood trickled from between his lips. Olan held his hand and willed his breathing to stop and for his pain to end as he stared into the man's stricken face. It seemed to take a long time for his breathing to finally stop, but in all reality, it may only have been a couple of minutes. He leaned down and put his ear to the man's chest and listened for a heartbeat. But there was nothing. He let his hand drop to the ground and stood up. He stood for a moment and tried to get his face under control. He didn't understand why this man's death seemed so much more tragic than any of the others he had witnessed, but somehow it was. Once he felt like he had his face and his emotions under control he turned away from the body and walked back to where he had left the pile of linens he had been tearing into bandages. A nice easy job like that was just what the doctor had ordered he decided as he sat back down on the ground next to the hospital tent. He picked up a large piece of cloth and began to tear it into strips while he tried to think of nothing in particular.

Roland was walking past when he saw him sitting there tearing bandages. Then he got a look at Olan's stricken face. He stopped and looked at him with concern.

"You look terrible. Is everything okay?" Olan shook his head.

"You know that man that just died under the tree?"

"Yeah, what about him?"

"I knew him from the orphanage where I grew up."

Roland reached out his hand and touched him on the shoulder in sympathy, "I am so sorry," he said.

Olan gave a small nod."I was wondering if it would be all right if I left a little early today. I am feeling a little out of it."

Roland nodded. "Of course. You have had a big shock and you should get some rest."

Olan gave him a weak smile of gratitude and stood up. "Thank you." He turned then and walked over to collect his horse. He mounted up and rode off in the direction of their camp in the woods with thoughts of the man Arian in his head. He was happy for him that he had been adopted and taken out of that awful place. He didn't blame him for what he had done all those years ago. They had all been children then and sometimes children could be cruel to one another. But everything had worked out for him and he had moved far beyond his time in the orphanage. He just felt bad that he had carried around this guilt for so many years.

Well at least he was at peace now he thought as he rode while tears rolled down his face that dripped off the end of his nose. What a waste. He wished now more than ever that this war could end so they could all go home again.

That evening, Prince Edward sat in his tent drinking brandy and thinking about the Welsh army. There was no doubt that his men were fighting hard and that there were at least double the number of English soldiers to Welsh ones, but the Welsh were turning out to be much more than they had bargained for. He didn't know how much longer they could hold out. He could see in the men's eyes that they were beginning to lose heart with the continuous viciousness of the Welsh.

Just then the tent flap opened, and he looked up to see Lord Edmond entering the tent. He gave the man a brief nod of acknowledgment and then continued to drink his brandy. Lord Edmond walked over to the table and sat down opposite the Prince. The light from the single candle that sat upon the table revealed the man's deeply lined face. In this light, he looked at least twice his age. He also looked very tired with dark circles under his eyes.

"Brandy?" he offered. Lord Edmond nodded and he poured him a cup. He took it gratefully and drank deeply. Then he put it down and wiped his mouth with the back of his hand.

"How are you doing, My Prince?" he asked.

Edward shook his head and took another sip of his brandy. "To be honest I grow tired of it all. The Welsh are turning out to be more of a force than we had prepared for even though we have the larger army."

Lord Edmond nodded his head in agreement. "Yes, they are very skilled and ferocious fighters." He agreed, taking another sip from his cup. Edward shrugged.

"I don't know anymore," he said. "Sometimes it just seems so futile. I am finding it harder and harder to get myself out of bed in the morning and do it all over again."

"I know what you mean." Lord Edmond said. "But we can't give up now. It wouldn't be right."

"What does it matter if it is right or not? I just want to go home in one piece."

"I understand, but we have to stick it out," Lord Edmond said consolingly. "I think we need to change our tactics. I feel it would make the men feel much more confident if you were to be the one to ride out at the head of the army from now on instead of myself or Sir Stanley."

"You two are much more skilled at this and more experienced than I am and that is why I have left you to lead the army."

"I know that, but now it is about morale. I know it would raise the men's spirits to have their Prince at the head of the army."

Edward shook his head. "I don't know. If this is about youthful leaders you are not that old yourself."

Lord Edmond smiled. "I am old enough that I am not a young man anymore. I am also not the Prince of England and you are. Trust me this will be a good thing."

Edward took a large sip from his cup while he thought about what the general was asking of him. He didn't want to lead the men. The person at the head of the army was most vulnerable and he didn't want to make himself an easy target. But he didn't know if he had any choice in the matter either.

"All right I will do it," he said as he looked into the older man's face. The general smiled again a little wider this time and his eyes seemed to twinkle for a second.

"Thank you, My Prince. I assure you this is a good thing you are doing," he said and draining his cup placed it back on the table. Then he stood and gave him a small bow before turning and leaving the tent once more.

After the general had left, he sat alone at the table for a few minutes while he finished his brandy. Then he stood up and blew out the single candle. Then he walked over to the sleeping cot in the corner and crawled beneath the blankets. As he lay there, he tried to compose his mind for sleep. He was worried about the next day even though he knew there was nothing he could do about it. He took a few deep breaths and closed his eyes. Then after a few minutes of deep breathing and forcing himself to think of nothing at all he managed to drift off to sleep.

The next morning Llywelyn and Owain awoke to snow. A fine dusting coated the ground, and small ice crystals hung from the branches of the trees they lay under. As the weather had grown colder and the sky had threatened snow, the three men had taken to sleeping under the trees for protection. Even so, their blankets were stiff with the cold and the two brothers jumped to their feet shivering. They rolled up their blankets and stuffed them into one of the saddlebags to keep them dry while they were gone.

"I wonder if his highness will let us sleep in his tent from now on?" Owain said between clenched teeth. He was shivering so badly that he was afraid he would knock out a tooth.

Olan already had a fire going and was cooking their breakfast.

The two brothers walked over to the fire and slowly began to warm a bit from the heat.

Olan handed them each a steaming cup of tea, and they took the cups gratefully. They both took a sip of tea and instantly felt warmer as the hot liquid trickled down their throats.

"Olan, you are a saint," Owain said bowing his head to him in deference. Olan and Llywelyn laughed and he cracked a grin. They ate a hasty breakfast and then pulled on their armor. They could see that the horses were already saddled and ready to go. Llywelyn smiled at Olan. He was always at least three steps ahead of them.

"Good luck," Olan said as the brothers mounted up.

"Thanks," Llywelyn said with another smile. They gave their horses a light kick then and rode off to join the rest of the army.

Olan watched as the brothers rode out of the clearing. He couldn't put his finger on it, but he had a bad feeling. Like something was going to happen that no one could stop. Owain had been very quiet last night as if there was something on his mind that he couldn't share. He knew that Llywelyn believed that his brother was back, but he still didn't feel like the same man to him that he had been before his imprisonment. Something was missing in him somehow. There was a hardness to him now that he had never had before. He would never say it out loud, but he didn't trust the man.

He put out the fire, and then picking up the saddlebags, placed them in the undergrowth between the trees that had not yet been touched by the snow and so was still bone dry. Then he saddled his horse and rode out of the clearing in the direction of the hospital tents.

The snow was much deeper once he had left the protection of the trees. It was well above his horse's hooves and was steadily getting deeper as he rode. It was going to be a cold wet day of fighting. He shivered just thinking about it. At least Llywelyn and his brother were on horseback which was something. But as for the foot soldiers, well he felt sorry for them. They were going to have an extremely hard time fighting as they struggled through the ever-growing snowdrifts.

Roland was sitting under a tree tearing cloth for dressings when he rode up. He dismounted and tied his horse's reins to a tree branch to keep him out of the weather to an extent. Roland saw him and stood up.

"Olan, there you are," he said with a smile.

"Hello, Roland," Olan said as he walked over to the man. "What can I help with?"

"Can you finish tearing up the bandages while I set up for the day?" Olan nodded and sat down under the tree. He picked up the pile of linens and began to tear them into strips in an almost meditative manner. He still couldn't shake off the feeling that something was wrong and that Owain was at the center of it all. He shook his head angrily. How could he be thinking so badly of the man? After all, he had been nothing but polite and pleasant towards him since his return. So why did he feel like something was about to happen that would involve the man? He bit his lip in frustration as he continued to tear bandages.

Meanwhile, out on the battlefield, the fighting was fierce and bloody as it had been so for the past several days. The snow had quickly turned from white to red as men fell to the many blades and arrows coming from all directions. Adrenalin was racing through his veins as Llywelyn rode through the fray using his sword to devastating effect. The snow was falling so thickly now that it was becoming harder and harder to see any farther than a foot in front of him. But still, he fought on.

Prince Edward rode out at the head of the English army as he had promised he would. The snow was making it hard to see and he wondered why they were doing this. He knew why his father wanted them to win, but this was insane. The visibility was so poor that they were just as likely to kill one of their own than the enemy. He shook his head though and just kept on fighting.

Then out of nowhere, he saw Llywelyn coming at him. His sword was covered in gore and his face was red with the adrenalin of the fight. But what was probably the most frightening thing about him was his eyes. They were the eyes of an animal and not a man. Their eyes met for a moment and then Llywelyn rode back into the fray. The moment their eyes had met however he had frozen. There had still been a mind behind the animalistic gaze. When he had seen that he had felt his blood run cold, there was no doubt in his mind that this was the most dangerous man alive.

Owain rode through the battle with his long sword out and was using it to good effect. From time to time he would catch glimpses of his brother and his uncle through the falling snow. He had to constantly shake it off his visor to see. Each time he saw his brother, he was taking down an English soldier with a ruthless look on his face. But then a second later his vision would be obscured once more by more snow on his visor. By the time he had shaken it off, his brother was gone again.

Each time he saw his brother taking down a soldier, he felt a swell of pride rise in him. He was so much like their father and wished that their father could have been here to see his son in action. He thought he would have been proud to see just how far Llywelyn had come over these past four years. But now thanks to Dafydd he was gone and would never see what his son had become. He suddenly felt anger well up in him and it came to him what he had to do. It was because of Dafydd's incompetence as a leader that they had not won this war. If the leadership had been left to his brother with Captain Carrol by his side, they would have defeated the English days ago. He sheathed his sword and took out his bow instead. Then he began to look for his uncle. It was time to end this.

As he searched for his uncle, he passed his brother and managed to send an arrow into the back of a man who was attempting to come at his brother from behind. It made him fall and he was trampled by Llywelyn's horse as he swung his sword at a soldier on horseback like himself. After a short time of searching, he found his uncle, and to his surprise, the man was completely unprotected. He shook the snow from his visor for what felt like the hundredth time and knocked an arrow to the string. He pulled it to his cheek and waited until his uncle was in just the right spot. Then he sent the arrow flying straight into his back. The arrow hit him with such force that it sent him flying off his horse onto the ground where he was immediately trampled by several horses.

He quickly put away his bow and pulled his sword back into his hand once more. Then he turned his horse's head around and holding his sword high yelled, "Dafydd is dead! They have killed our Prince!" Several of the soldiers heard him and took up the cry in turn.

Llywelyn heard the cry and looked around in surprise. He couldn't see his uncle anywhere. Though he thought it might have something to do with the falling snow. He looked back in time to see a man trying to come at him from the side. He cut the man down and then continued to look for his uncle. He saw his brother first though. Owain came riding towards him fighting for all he was worth.

"What is going on?" he called to his brother.

"Dafydd is dead," Owain called back.

"What?"

"I saw it happen. He was hit from behind by an arrow which made him fall off his horse where he was then trampled to death." Just then a man on horseback came at him from the side on the left. Owain hit him in the chest with the flat of his blade hard enough to send him flying off his horse where he was then trampled to death once he hit the ground.

"Good work," Llywelyn said as he leaned down and decapitated a man who was trying to shoot him with an arrow.

"Thanks," Owain said killing another man who was trying to come at him from behind.

"I will have to tell Carrol. He will have to lead us now," Llywelyn said panting.

Owain put away his sword and pulled out his bow once more.

"Carrol is a good soldier, but he is not a leader," he said shooting a man in the chest who was about to charge his brother killing him where he sat. The man's lifeless body teetered in place for a moment and then fell to the ground. The riderless horse screamed in fright and galloped away.

"I am sure he will do fine," Llywelyn said killing a man coming at him from the right side. Owain shook his head.

"No, he won't, and you know it. We need a real leader. We need you. Why can't you see that?" Llywelyn glared at his brother.

"We are not having this conversation here."

Owain glared back at him in return. "Face it Llywelyn, you were born to lead. Everyone follows you." Llywelyn swung his sword in a backward swing and killed a man coming at him from behind.

"I don't want to do this," he said.

"I know, but we need you. Please, Llywelyn." He gave his brother a pleading look. Llywelyn shrugged and nodded grudgingly.

"All right, I will do it. Find Carrol and tell him what has happened," he said. Owain smiled at him and rode away to find the captain.

Carrol was leading a band of archers when he heard the cry of vengeance for the Prince's death. He turned to one of the archers to ask if he knew what was going on when he saw Owain riding towards him. He waved to the man as he came closer.

"What is going on?" he asked as Owain reached him.

"Dafydd is dead," he said.

"What?"

"It is true. I saw him fall myself," Owain said. "Llywelyn is taking on the leadership of the army. I need you to keep an eye on him and watch his back. Here, you can take my horse." He jumped down off the horse and gave the reins to Carrol. Carrol took them and mounted up. Then he rode away to find Llywelyn.

He found him very quickly and rode towards him just in time to see him rays his bloody sword high for all to see. As he rode closer he saw the man's face set in determination as he opened his mouth and called out loud enough for all to hear,

"To me! To me!" like magic the Welsh army seemed to turn and flock to him like ducklings to a mother swan. He rode to Llywelyn's side as he began the charge.

It was over very quickly. As soon as Edward saw Llywelyn riding towards him at the head of the Welsh army he knew they were finished. Their eyes met briefly and what he saw in those eyes was enough to chill him to the bone. He knew without any doubt that he was a dead man if he kept fighting. He signaled to Lord William to abandon the fight. Lord William nodded in acquiescence seeing the look on the Prince's face. He relayed the message to his officers who sent the message back through the ranks of soldiers. It was time to go.

Llywelyn saw the English begin to retreat and called off the attack. His brother, having managed to get another horse, came riding up to him with a smile on his face.

"You did well," he said when he reached his brother. Llywelyn nodded in thanks. His throat was dry from yelling and he couldn't talk. All the adrenalin had left him now and his arms felt like they were made of lead. He didn't think he could raise his sword again for several days even if his life depended on it. He wished for a moment that his father could have been here to see the English retreating. Maybe he was in a way. He was and always would be in his heart and so where he went his father did also. With one last look at the retreating backs of their enemies, he gave the signal to disperse. Then he turned his horse's head and rode away from the battlefield followed closely by his brother. They had done it. They had won and now they could go home. He knew it was a good thing he had done. His brother grinned at him with pride along with Carrol and the other officers who rode with him away from the battlefield. So why then did this victory feel like ashes in his mouth?

Chapter 18

Terms of Surrender

Meanwhile, back at the hospital tents, Olan was dressing a man's injured arm when he began to notice the conversation going on around him. For most of the day, he had been focused on the job at hand and trying not to look for Llywelyn among the injured being brought in for treatment. It had been how he had kept himself from going crazy with worry for his friend.

"Did you see him?" the young soldier to his left asked the group at large. At least ten men lay on the ground around the hospital tent in varying stages of injury. The man to his left was young, no more than 17 with short blond hair, blue eyes, and had the same thin tired look about him that they all had after days of fighting. He had a ragged cut down one cheek that Roland had managed to stitch up, but he would still have a scar. He also had his left arm in a sling to keep him from moving it after he had dislocated it during the battle.

"How could you miss him holding his sword up like that like a flag? All be it a bloody one," the man Olan was tending said. He was slightly older than the man to his left but only by a couple of years. His hair was dark brown and was matted to his head with sweat and dirt. His eyes were a deep green and very large in his rather pale face. "The way he called us to him was something I will never forget." There was a murmur of agreement among the men at this.

"What happened?" Olan asked as he wrapped a bandage around the man's arm. The man sucked in his breath in pain as he pulled the bandage tight. "Sorry." He mumbled as he tied it off. The man shook his head as best he could. His face gleamed with cold sweat and had grown even paler. Making his eyes stand out even more in his face.

"We won," the man to his left said with a grin.

"How did that happen?" Olan asked holding a cup of water laced with brandy to the soldier's lips. He drank half the cup before turning his head away unable to speak from the pain in his arm.

The young man to his left looked at him with a large grin on his face. "We won," he said with pride.

"How did that happen?" Olan asked turning to the man.

"It was Lord Llywelyn. We could never have done it without him," another man said his face glowing with pride.

"I thought Dafydd was leading the Welsh army?" Olan said confused.

"He was," the man to his left confirmed. "But something happened to him in the middle of all the fighting and so it was left to Lord Llywelyn to lead us. I will always remember him coming, riding out of the middle of all the fighting with his sword covered in blood and gore. The sword raised above his head as he called us to his side." There was another murmur of agreement among the group of soldiers.

"I can imagine," Olan said turning back to the man with the injured arm. He could imagine it all too clearly. People had always followed him without question. That man was a born leader. He just couldn't see it himself. He checked the soldier's vital signs and found them strong. His pulse was light, and his face was beginning to gain back some color to it.

"How do you feel?" he asked placing a hand on the man's shoulder.

"Terrible," the man replied. He smiled at him in sympathy.

"Your arm will hurt for a time, but I promise it won't last forever. Just try not to use that arm for a couple of days while it heals." The man nodded as best he could and closed his eyes. Olan stood up then and looked for Roland. He spotted him over by the supply wagon and walked over to him.

"Ah, Olan, how are you?" he asked holding a water skin to his horse's lips while it drank.

"I should go. Do you think you can handle things without me?" Olan asked. Roland nodded and smiled.

"Of course," he said. "Go and tend to Lord Llywelyn. I am sure he will be dead tired after such a victory." Olan gave the man a quick smile of thanks and walked over to his horse. He untied his reins and mounting up rode off to find Llywelyn and his brother.

When he reached the camp in the woods, he found the brothers already there. They each held two saddlebags which they proceeded to attach to their saddles.

"What is going on?" Olan asked confused.

"Llywelyn is now the leader of the army and so the officers have insisted that we take the command tent," Owain explained tightening the final buckle of his saddlebags.

"I heard something about that from some of the injured men at the hospital tents. So you really are the new leader?" Llywelyn shrugged.

"Of the army," Owain smiled at his brother.

"You are funny brother," he said. Llywelyn shrugged again too tired to argue. Then they all mounted up and rode off in the direction of the command tent.

They reached it a short time later and were greeted warmly by the guards. They dismounted and Olan took all three horses to be housed with the rest of the animals. The two brothers were ushered inside where supper was already on the table. They pulled up chairs and sat down to eat. Owain looked at his brother as they ate and saw how tired he was.

"You should get some sleep," he said when Llywelyn had finished eating.

"That would be nice," he said standing up. "What about you?"

"I will sleep in a bit." Llywelyn nodded and climbed onto the camp bed. Pausing only long enough to remove his boots before lying down and falling to sleep the second his head hit the pillow.

Owain sat at the table drinking a cup of brandy and watching his brother sleeping. He longed for sleep. His body was aching with fatigue and he could barely keep himself upright in his chair. But his mind refused to settle. So he sat there drinking his brandy and thinking about the future. He hoped that his brother would come to his senses and see that he was truly the leader they all needed. People followed him without question because they believed in him as he was already their leader. But for some inexplicable reason, he just couldn't seem to see the truth for himself. He hoped that in time that would change because he knew in his heart that without Llywelyn they were doomed to fail.

Meanwhile, in the English camp, Prince Edward also sat in his tent drinking brandy. He was going over the battle in his mind. He couldn't get the image of the warrior Llywelyn out of his mind. He had seemed like something out of legend with the way he used his sword and the look he had born upon his face as he oh so casually cut down the English soldiers that stood in his path. They were both of a similar age, but the look in the man's eyes when their eyes had met showed intelligence and resolve that spoke of someone much older.

Just then the tent flap opened, and Lord Edmond entered the tent. He walked over to the table and sat down across from the Prince. He poured himself a cup of brandy from the decanter on the table and took a sip while looking at Edward with concern.

"Are you all right?" he asked. "You look a little shaky." Edward shrugged and took another sip from his cup.

"I am as well as I can be I suppose." Lord Edmond smiled at the young Prince.

"I understand what you mean," the older man said taking another couple of sips from his cup.

"I mean how am I supposed to go home to my father and tell him that we lost to an army half the size of our own? We are supposed to be strong and fierce, but thanks to that man we were made to look a fool out there on the battlefield."

Lord Edmond nodded in understanding. "It isn't your fault," he said sympathetically.

"No, but I was in charge wasn't I? If so, it will be my fault we failed in the eyes of the army and the crown." Edward said miserably.

Lord Edmond took a sip from his cup and then placed it back on the table. "Look," he said looking the Prince in the face. "War is a fickle thing at the best of times. Sometimes you win and sometimes you lose. There is no shame in that."

"Sure," Edward said unconvinced.

"You know your father has lost a battle or two in his time, and so have I. So has Sir Stanley for that matter. You are not alone in this."

"Really, my father has lost battles?"

"Yes, plenty. Like I said it is all a part of war." He smiled at the look of relief on the Prince's face. He was happy he had been able to soothe the young man's feelings of guilt. He picked up his cup once more and took a healthy sip and then cleared his throat. "I have actually come here to discuss what we should do next. Personally,

I don't see there is much we can do. We can't change the fact that the Welsh won."

Edward nodded and drained the last drops from his cup. "Well, I can't go back to my father without having come to some kind of understanding with them first," he said.

"I agree," Lord Edmond said draining his own cup.

"What do you suggest," Edward asked the older man.

"We must send a message to their leader to come and discuss terms of surrender that will benefit both of our lands," Lord Edmond said simply. Edward nodded in agreement.

"Do you think that young man is still their leader?"

"Do you mean the one holding his bloody sword up like a flag with the look of fire in his eye?" Edward nodded. "Yes, I believe he is their leader."

"Do you know his name or any information at all about him?"

"No, but I am sure Sir Stanley would. Would you like me to go and find him for you and bring him here?"

Edward shook his head. "Maybe in the morning. At the moment all I want is to crawl into bed and sleep." The older man smiled at him.

"Of course. I will leave you and return in the morning with Sir Stanley," Lord Edmond said standing up. He turned then and left the tent, leaving the Prince alone with his thoughts once more.

Edward stood up and walking over to the bed sat down to remove his shoes. Then he crawled under the blankets without bothering to undress and fell fast asleep the moment his head hit the pillow.

About three days later, Llywelyn and his brother Owain were sitting in the command tent eating breakfast at the table when they heard a commotion outside the tent.

"What's going on?" Owain said looking towards the tent flap.

"I don't know," Llywelyn replied putting down his fork and standing up. He left the tent with his brother close behind him to see what the commotion was all about.

The moment they walked outside, they saw the guards had circled a young man who looked both afraid and defiant.

Llywelyn walked up to the closest guard and stopped. "What is going on here?" he demanded asking the guard. The man gave him a small bow of the head.

"This man is an Englishman who says he has a message for you from his Prince," he scoffed.

"What makes you think he is lying?" The man gave a snort of derision.

"He is an Englishman."

"So that automatically makes him a liar?" The man looked away from him and shook his head. He did at least have the grace to blush with something like shame.

"Let him through," Llywelyn ordered. The guards reluctantly parted to let the man through. As he reached Llywelyn and Owain they saw just how young he truly was. He had to be no more than 16 or 17 and carried no weapons on him. Not even the common dagger that most people carried on them at all times. He had bright blond hair and dark blue eyes that seemed too large for his thin face.

"You wished to see me?" Llywelyn said looking into the young man's face. He nodded once but still wouldn't speak.

"I think all these guards make him nervous," Owain observed. Llywelyn smiled at the young man.

"I think you are right," he said. Another guard piped up then.

"I do not think it advisable for you to meet with this man alone, My Lord." The man said concerned. Llywelyn turned to the guard and shook his head.

"He is unarmed and half the size of both myself and my brother. I think we are more than capable of handling the situation ourselves." He turned his back on the guards then and beckoned the young man inside the tent.

Owain sat down on the cot and watched the young man as he sat down at the table across from Llywelyn. He looked slightly less afraid now that he was away from all the guards.

"Brandy?" Llywelyn offered. The man nodded his head.

"Yes, thank you," he said. Llywelyn poured him a cup from the decanter on the table and handed it to the man. The man lifted the cup to his mouth and took a sip, and then a second. Llywelyn watched him as he drank and waited to hear the Prince's message.

"Does the Prince of England have a message for me?" he asked as the man lowered his cup to the table once more. He nodded.

"Yes," he said pulling a folded and sealed piece of parchment from the pocket of his cloak. Llywelyn poured himself a cup of brandy and took a drink and then put his cup back on the table as the young messenger slid the sealed message across the table to him.

"Is this his message then?" The man nodded in reply and picked up his cup once more and took a drink. Llywelyn broke the seal and unfolding the message began to read. He read it through twice before putting it down.

"What does it say?" Owain asked. Llywelyn didn't answer, but handed him the message to read himself. Then he looked back at the young messenger.

"Is that all?" he asked looking the young man in the eyes. The man blinked and looked away.

"Yes," he said picking up his cup and draining it in one gulp. "Will you come?" Llywelyn nodded.

"This afternoon," he said. "I am bringing some people with me. It would be foolish for me to meet with him alone." The man nodded and stood up.

"I will tell him you are coming," he said and turning left the tent once more.

"You know I am coming with you," Owain said standing up and walking over to the table. He sat down in the vacated chair across from his brother and looked him in the face with determination.

"I wouldn't want anyone else," Llywelyn assured him. Owain gave him a small smile.

"I think Carrol should be there as well." Llywelyn nodded. "We must make this on our terms and not his. He is the one surrendering not us." Llywelyn nodded again.

"I know," he said. Just then the tent flap opened, and Olan entered the tent.

"I just saw a young Englishman riding away in the direction of the English army," he said walking over to them.

"He came to deliver a message from their Prince," Llywelyn explained. He picked up the message and handed it to Olan. Olan read it over and then looked up at the two brothers.

"Will you go?"

"Yes, and I am bringing Owain and Carrol with me." Olan nodded in approval.

"Good idea. You shouldn't meet these people alone," he said.

"I want you with me as well as a witness." Olan nodded again.

"Of course," he said.

"Can you go and find Carrol and bring him here?"

"Right away," Olan said and left the tent to find the captain. Llywelyn drained his cup and stood up. He walked over to the chest and finding a hairbrush began to tidy his hair as best as he could. He hadn't washed it in days, and it was sticking up in all directions. Owain watched his preparations with a small smile on his face.

"What?" Llywelyn said defiantly.

"Nothing," Owain said his smile widening.

"What?"

"Only a leader would be concerned about his appearance when going to meet the leader of the opposition." Llywelyn glared at his brother.

"I grow weary of your conviction that I am this great leader."

"I only say it because it is the truth. I just wish you could see it for yourself," Owain said.

"You are living in a dream world," Llywelyn said placing the brush back in the chest. "Carrol will be here soon enough."

Olan returned a short time later with the captain, and after discussing the strategy to use with the Prince, they mounted up and the four men rode of in the direction of the English camp.

As they rode, Llywelyn found himself thinking about what his brother had said. If he was honest with himself, he was scared to admit his natural leadership. The last thing he wanted was to become the leader of Gwynedd. It was a responsibility that he couldn't take on. No matter what his brother thought. He was too young and inexperienced.

"But are you?" a small voice inside his head seemed to say. He shook a finger at the voice and tried to focus on the task ahead as they came in sight of the English camp.

Chapter 19

A Long Road Home

As they reached the English camp, Llywelyn and his men were stopped by the English sentries.

"State your name and purpose," one of the sentries said. He was an older man with receding gray hair and beady little eyes that watered in the sunlight. Llywelyn simply held out the Prince's message and waited while the man read it over.

"Go ahead," he said waving them on. Llywelyn nodded briefly in thanks and rode on into the camp with the others following behind him.

The first thing he noticed was the hectic nature of the camp. Everyone was busy doing something. There was no laughter amongst the men as they worked at packing, tending the animals, and the various other chores involved with striking camp.

"I think I see the command tent," Owain said riding up beside his brother and pointing off in the distance to their right. Craning his neck, Llywelyn saw the English flag atop a tent that was so large it seemed to dominate over the camp as a whole.

"I think you are right," he agreed, turning his horse's head rode in the direction of the English command tent with his brother beside him, and Olan and Carrol following behind.

As they reached the ring of guards surrounding the tent, they dismounted. Llywelyn explained who they were, and they were waved through into the tent beyond.

Edward was sitting at the table in the middle of the command tent with Lord Edmond and Sir Stanley on either side of him as they entered the tent. He looked around at the sound of their footsteps and seeing who it was waved them to seats on the other side of the table. There were only three seats though, so Olan was forced to sit on the sleeping cot in the corner instead. Llywelyn sat down at the table and his brother and army captain sat down on either side of him, mirroring the Prince and his men across the table.

"I see you got my message, Lord Llywelyn," the Prince said avoiding direct eye contact with the man. He was nervous to look him in the eyes after what he had seen there the last time he had dared to do so.

"Yes, I did," Llywelyn confirmed. "This is my brother Owain, and my army captain Carrol," he said pointing first to his brother and then to Carrol in turn. "I have also brought along my man-servant as a witness to our conversation here today." The Prince nodded his head in understanding.

"This is my father's general, Lord Edmond, and his best knight, Sir Stanley," he said pointing to each man in turn. Sir Stanley cleared his throat to speak.

"I can not honestly say it is a pleasure to see you two again, but I am happy we are doing so on more civil terms than those of a battlefield," he said.

"I assure you the last thing I want is more fighting," Llywelyn said looking directly at the knight.

Sir Stanley nodded and looked away.

"Can I offer you and your men something to drink?" Edward asked.

"No thank you," Llywelyn said. He wanted to get this over with as quickly as possible. There was something about being surrounded by all these Englishman that was making his skin crawl and jump with nervous tension despite the fact that they had come in peace.

"Very well then," Edward said settling himself more comfortably in his chair. "You know why you are here?"

Llywelyn nodded. "You wish to discuss terms of surrender," he said in as neutral a voice as he could manage.

"Yes, I do," Edward said taking a deep breath. He saw out of the corner of his eye both Lord Edmond and Sir Stanley give him nods of encouragement.

"Right," he said shifting uncomfortably in his seat. Llywelyn was making him extremely nervous. Even though he knew the man was a similar age to himself he seemed much more confident and controlled than his age would suggest. He took a deep breath and continued. "I have with the help of Lord Edmond and Sir Stanley here begun to write up some terms. Sir Stanley handed him the papers and he slid them across the table. Llywelyn picked them up and began to read. Edward watched him as he read and tried to detect any kind of emotion from the man as he read the terms, but his face remained blank and expressionless.

He finished reading and passed the papers to his brother before looking back at the Prince.

"From what I have read here, it all looks good," he said.

"I am sure you will have some requests of your own," Edward said. Llywelyn nodded.

"Only one," he said. Edward looked at him in surprise.

"Just one?"

"I want you to assure me that you will not attempt to invade our land again and leave us in peace."

"I can not speak for my father, but I can assure you that I won't be attempting any such thing on your land myself," Edward assured him.

"I want your word that your kingdom will stay away from mine."

"What will you do for us in return?" Sir Stanley asked.

"In return?"

"If we are going to petition the King to agree with your terms we need to present him with something that will benefit us as well." Lord Edmond nodded in agreement.

"We have shown you how strong we are as both a nation and an army. I am sure the King will want the fighting to stop," Owain said putting down the papers.

"He will need something more than that I think," Sir Stanley said.

"What would satisfy the King?" Llywelyn asked looking directly at the knight.

"A written promise that your people will stop raiding the English border." Llywelyn looked to his brother to see his reaction. Owain shrugged and shook his head as if to say, "Up to you little brother." Llywelyn gave him a "Thanks for nothing," look and turned back to face the Prince and his men.

"I will make sure the raiding on your border stops if you can assure me that your king will leave our land in peace," he said.

"That seems fair," Edward said. Both Sir Stanley and Lord Edmond nodded their heads in approval. Edward passed Llywelyn a quill and a bottle of ink. Llywelyn unstoppered the bottle and dipping the end of the quill in the ink began to write at the bottom of the page his terms and his promise to stop the raiding of the English border. Then he signed his name and handed the paper, ink, and quill to the Prince who did the same.

"Well, I think we are done here. Unless there is anything else you wanted to talk about?" Edward shook his head.

"No that was all."

"All right then." Llywelyn stood up then followed by his brother and Carrol. Seeing that they were about to leave Olan stood up from where he had been sitting on the sleeping cot and followed the three men out of the tent once more.

After Llywelyn and his men had left the tent, Edward turned to Lord Edmond and Sir Stanley.

"Well I think that went well," he said. The two older men nodded in agreement.

"You handled things beautifully, My Prince." Sir Stanley said with a smile. Lord Edmond nodded again.

"Yes, you did. You would have made your father proud if he had been here to see it," he said. Edward felt shy from all the compliments.

"We should get packing. It is a long road home," he said. The two older men nodded once more and stood up. They gave the Prince one last smile of appreciation and left the tent.

Once they had left, the Prince walked over to the bed and stripped it. Packing the blankets into the trunk that sat in the corner, along with the cups from the table as well as the brandy decanter. The table, chairs bed, and trunk would be left in the tent when they took it down and put it on one of the wagons. He sat down on the now-empty bed and thought about his father. He didn't know how he would take the news that they had failed. He didn't think he would be as calm about it as the others believed. This had been his first mission as the future leader of England, and he had failed. How could he face him? He placed his head in his hands and tried to clear his mind of all thought. He knew there was no sense in worrying about his father's response until he saw him. But it wasn't easy. He had never wanted anything more than his father's approval, and now he didn't know if that was a possibility anymore.

A few hours later, Llywelyn stood with his brother and Captain Carrol watching the English leave.

"It will be good to see the back of them," Carrol said as several wagons pulled by horses rolled past. Reminding them all of the true vastness of the English army.

"It is still hard to believe we beat them, to be honest," Llywelyn said. Owain smiled at his brother.

"It was all because of you," he said. Carrol nodded.

"Yes." He agreed. Llywelyn shrugged and turned back to watch the cavalry riding past. As the Prince rode past flanked on either side by Sir Stanley and Lord Edmond, their eyes met for just a moment before he turned his head away and disappeared among his soldiers. He sighed in relief. It was all over and now they could go home. He missed his brothers and his mother and all the small comforts of the castle such as a warm bed and blazing fireplaces and Elsa's cooking. He turned to his brother.

"Let's go home," he said. Owain nodded.

"Yes," he said, and with that they turned as one and walked back to their camp to begin packing up for the travel home.

Aberfraw Castle

Dafydd, having just returned from a trip into town to see the market, was in the stables when his brother Rhodri found him. He took one look at his brother's face and knew something bad had happened.

"What's wrong?" he asked. Rhodri squared his shoulders and took a deep breath.

"It is mother, she has taken a turn for the worst I fear," he said trying with great effort to keep from breaking down.

"Lead the way," Dafydd said and they left the stables together. Dafydd's heart was racing with fear. What if she was already dead and he never had a chance to say goodbye. He wished his brother Llywelyn was here. It broke his heart a little to know that their mother would never see her two eldest sons again before she died. But there was nothing to be done. Owain was in England as far as they knew, and Llywelyn was at war with the English, and who knew when he would return. He couldn't bring himself to think that he wouldn't. His brother was too strong and too good a fighter not to return after the war was over.

With these thoughts in his head, he walked into the castle and through the halls to his mother's room, hoping all the while that she was still alive. He didn't know what he would do if she died. It was hard enough that his father was gone. In a way, his father had been gone for years ever since he had been taken away to prison in England. But to lose their mother as well was a blow he didn't think he could bear. He was not yet a man and didn't think he could run things while his brother and uncle were away. He didn't know the first thing about running a castle let alone an entire kingdom. Fraught with anxiety, he pushed open his mother's door and stepped inside with Rhodri at his side.

He crossed the room to his mother's bedside and looked down at her. For a moment he thought she was already dead, but then she opened her eyes. She smiled at the sight of her two youngest sons.

"Dafydd, Rhodri, please sit down." The two boys sat down on opposite sides of the bed facing their mother. "I am so happy you are here."

"Are you all right mother?" Dafydd asked. She smiled at him lovingly.

"I will be," she said. "Have you heard from your brother?"

"No, not a word," Dafydd replied looking into her thin pale face. He could see all the bones in her face and the hands that lay upon the blanket were like those of a skeleton.

"That is too bad. I would have liked to have seen him one last time," she said with a small sigh.

"What do you mean?" Dafydd asked feeling overly concerned now.

"I am dying. It won't be long now. I am simply happy to have you both by my side," she said.

"Are you really dying?" Rhodri asked.

"Yes, but at least I will be with your father again soon. Be good you two and listen to your brother," she admonished.

"We will mother, we promise," Dafydd said, tears welling up in his eyes. Rhodri nodded without speaking.

"I love you both, and tell your brother the same for me." They both nodded wordlessly. She took one long breath in and let it out, and then a second and then breathed no more. Tears rained down the boys' faces as they looked down at the face of their dead mother in shock. After a moment, they looked at each other and slid off the bed at the same time and wordlessly left the bed-chamber together.

A few nights later, somewhere in the middle of Gwynedd, Llywelyn woke suddenly with the feeling like there was something wrong. The tent was pitch black, and he could hear the sound of his brother's and Olan's deep breathing beside him. He listened hard to see if he could hear anything outside the confines of the tent, but he couldn't hear anything. He shook himself and stood up. Feeling the sudden need to go to the bathroom he slid out from under the blankets and slipping on his boots left the tent as quietly as possible.

Outside the stars were so bright in the sky that he blinked in surprise at the bright light. A half-moon shone its muted light down on the crisp new snow that had fallen during the night and made it shine like crystal. He walked a short distance into the trees and pulling down his leggings relieved himself against a tree. The forest was dead quiet and felt almost lifeless. Even though he knew it was full of creatures both big and small.

He still couldn't shake the feeling of unease though as he pulled up his leggings once more and turned to head back to the tent. Maybe it was anxiety about what he might find when he returned to the castle. He had been gone for so long that the place felt almost unreal to him. Like something from a dream or a distant memory. If he was feeling like this after being away for a few months, he couldn't imagine what his brother was feeling when he had been away from the place for several years.

With these thoughts in his head, he walked back to the tent. He stopped at the entrance and took one last look at the surrounding Welsh encampment and wondered how he had ended up here. He had never wanted to lead these men and yet he had been forced into the role by circumstance. Now he was going home at the head of the conquering army and was yet again left without any choice but to step into his uncle's shoes once again and become the ruler of Gwynedd. He shook his head in resignation and walked back inside the tent once more.

Chapter 20

Return of The Prodigal

It took several weeks of travel for the whole of the English army to leave Gwynedd and cross the border back into England once more. Each night, Edward would lay down to sleep on his cot in the command tent only to find himself waking from yet another nightmare a few hours later. Different images from the final battle kept coming back to him as he rode at the head of the army each day, and would haunt his dreams at night. Sometimes it was the memories of the fighting itself, and other times it was the sight of Llywelyn's face when he held his bloody sword high like a banner as he called his men to his side. Then other times, it was the sight of so many dead bodies upon the snow, turning it from white to crimson with their blood.

One morning after the army had left the border far behind, Lord Edmond entered the command tent to find the Prince already starring into a cup of brandy that he held in his hands. He walked over to the table and sat down opposite the Prince.

"Well, we are getting close," he said picking up the decanter and pouring a healthy dose into a second cup. He placed the decanter back on the table and then took a long drink from his cup. He savored the taste as the brandy trickled down the back of his throat, filling him up with heat as it hit his stomach and spread through his bloodstream.

"Are we?" the Prince said. "In all honesty, I haven't been paying attention to where we are since crossing the border."

"In my estimate, I would say we are no more than two weeks away from Winchester," Lord Edmond said taking another sip from his cup.

"Oh, good," Edward said distractedly. He had another sleepless night and was still not fully awake. Lord Edmond noticed the Prince's air of detachment and looked more closely at his face. He had dark circles under his eyes from his lack of sleep and he was very pale.

"Are you all right, My Prince?" he asked concerned at what he saw.

"I'm all right," Edward said stifling a yawn.

"Bad dreams?" Lord Edmond said with a fatherly smile. Edward looked at him in surprise.

"How did you know?" he asked. Lord Edmond's smile grew wider as he looked the Prince in the eyes.

"We all have them from time to time. It is a part of being a soldier," he said.

"Really?"

"Really."

"So I will always have these dreams?"

The older man smiled, his eyes twinkling, "They get better over time. It is best to talk about them if you can."

Edward nodded. "Thanks. I will think about it."

"We need to pack up and start moving, or we will never get home."

Edward smiled for what felt like the first time in years. "Sure," he said and downed the last of his brandy.

A short time later, the army began to move. Edward was once again on his horse at the head of the army with Sir Stanley and Lord Edmond on either side of him. He wasn't quite ready to share his dreams with anyone, but he was happy to know he would have someone he could talk to when he was ready. Throughout the war in Wales, he had grown to trust the general and felt like he could confide in him when the time came. There was something solid and comforting about the older man. He had fought in many battles and seen so much more than Edward thought he ever would. Sir Stanley was just as old and just as battle worn, but he didn't exactly exude comfort. He was much more taciturn and was more likely to say something harsh and discriminating than helpful. He hoped that he would never become bitter like the knight. He hoped that he would be much more like the general when he was their age, willing to lend a helping hand to some young soldier who was having nightmares from the things he had seen on the field of battle.

Winchester Castle, Chester, England

Two weeks later...

Prince Edward rode up to the gates of Winchester Castle with a heavy heart. The dark circles under his eyes were still there, and his face had a haunted look to it. He still hadn't been able to find it in himself to share his dreams with the general, and so his nights were still very unsettled. He was also fraught with anxiety about the prospect of telling his father that they had lost to the much smaller Welsh army. In the past, they had relied on the fear of their formidable size to gain the advantage of their enemies. But now if the news were to get out that they had been defeated in Wales by a much smaller army that scare tactic would become useless for future military engagements.

On his left rode Lord Edmond, and on his right rode Sir Stanley. They didn't look much better. Looking at their respective faces he was reminded just how old they were. On the battlefield, they had seemed like two young men in their prime: swift and agile in their every movement. Now they looked like what they were two old men, battle-worn and weary. It had been a slow and somewhat somber journey what with the several different sections of the army traveling together. The cavalry had tried their best to match the speed of the foot soldiers, which had meant travel had gone much slower than if they had separated. Once they reached their destination the army had dispersed, each man for his own home with Edward and his two companions riding alone to Winchester Castle.

They reached the castle gates and were admitted by two burly guards who gave a respectful nod of greeting to both Sir Stanley and Lord Edmond and gave the Prince a low bow. They rode through the gates into the courtyard, where they dismounted. A young stable boy took their horses for them and led them off in the direction of the royal stables. Together the three men walked up to the front doors of the castle, which were opened by yet another guard. Once the doors had closed firmly behind them Edward turned to the two older men.

"I have to find my father and tell him what has happened." Lord Edmond nodded.

"We will come with you," he said. Sir Stanley nodded his head in agreement.

"Thank you." Edward said in complete sincerity. He knew then that they had his back not only in battle, but in everything that mattered. They turned then as one and went to find the King.

They found the King a short time later in his room. By this point Edward's stomach was so tied up in knots of anxiety that he couldn't bring himself to knock on the door. Seeing his distress, Lord Edmond gave him a reassuring smile and knocked instead. The King called from inside the room, and opening the door he led the way inside. Sir Stanley, and a weak kneed Edward following behind him.

The King was sitting at the table in the corner writing when they entered the room. He looked up and smiled when he saw who it was. He put down his quill and closed his ink well to keep the ink from drying out before standing up to greet them.

"I had heard rumors that the army had returned. It looks like the rumors were right," he said looking the three men over. He noted the dark circles under their eyes and the general air of exhaustion and all three faces. "Rough journey?"

They all nodded.

"It was all rough. It is good to be home once more." Lord Edmond said in reply.

"Then by all means please sit and have a cup of wine. It will warm your bellies after your long journey." The three men nodded in unison and sat down at the table. The King sat back down, and picking up the decanter that sat in the middle of the table, filled three cups with wine before topping up his own cup in turn.

"Thank you, Your Majesty." Lord Edmond said taking a sip from his cup.

"Yes, thank you." Sir Stanley said doing the same. The Prince still unable to speak gave a jerky little nod of thanks.

The King looked at his son closely for the first time since the three men had entered the room. He noted his son's pale face and the dark circles under his eyes. As well as his haunted look and the fear that was not hidden very deep behind his eyes. He wondered just what he had seen or done during the campaign to give him such a look.

"So tell me, where do things stand with the Welsh?" Edward shifted uncomfortably in his seat. Lord Edmond took the lead once more to spare the young Prince yet more distress and looked the King in the face as he spoke.

"I am sorry to say we lost the war in the final battle," the general said not taking his eyes from the king's face.

"What?"

"It is true Your Majesty." Sir Stanley piped up.

"It was close for a long time!" Lord Edmond continued. "The Welsh were strong fighters and held their own despite their much smaller size." The King raised his eyebrows.

"Then what happened? Why did a much smaller army manage to beat the whole of the formidable English army?" he demanded, trying his best to not lose his temper at such news.

"Well, I think it all went south when Dafydd fell in battle," the general said.

"Dafydd was killed?" the King said shocked.

"Yes, it was during the final battle in fact," Sir Stanley said. The King looked at his son who was still not speaking. The Prince gave a short nod at the king's look and stared into his cup of wine to avoid eye contact.

"Yes, and then after he fell, his nephew Llywelyn took up the fight and rallied the Welsh soldiers around him," Lord Edmond said taking up the tale. "It was something to see."

"When Llywelyn rode out in front of the Welsh army with his bloody sword held high like some kind of banner, his men came to him. It was a sight I will never forget." Sir Stanley said with a small shiver. The Prince and the general nodded in agreement at the knight's words.

"Is that all?" the King asked a little irritated at their feeble reasons for such a defeat.

Edward took one last fortifying swallow of wine and then put the cup back on the table. Taking a deep breath he looked his father in the eye for the first time since he had entered the room.

"No, that's not all of it," he said quietly. His heart was beating a million miles a minute and he could feel his stomach roiling in painful knots of anxiety, but he didn't break the king's gaze.

"I talked to Lord Llywelyn," he said.

"What did he have to say?"

"We discussed terms of surrender. I have the written account here with me." Edward reached into his pocket and handed his father the written account of his talk with the man. The King opened it and read it through twice before putting it down.

"What made you think you had the authority to make such an agreement?" the King said with a glare.

"I had no choice if I was going to get us all out of there alive. The terms seemed more than fair. He would let us go without pursuit if we agreed not to return and wage battle on their land again," he said with a glare of his own.

"He is right." Lord Edmond spoke up before the King had a chance to speak. Sir Stanley nodded his head in agreement.

"I am King here."

"You weren't there. You didn't look into the man's eyes and see your fate written there," Edward protested.

"The man is formidable even at such a young age. I think Edward did very well," Sir Stanley said in the Prince's defense. The King shook his head and changed the subject.

"So Llywelyn is the new leader of Gwynedd now?" he said.

"I don't know if he is the permanent new leader or not. I think he was just standing in for Lord Dafydd," Edward said taking a sip of wine.

"Well?"

"Well, what?" Edward asked taking another sip of wine.

"What are you going to do about him?" the King asked looking directly into his son's face. Edward put down his cup and squared his shoulders.

"I don't believe it is my job to do anything about the man. I am not King here you are," he said defiantly. Lord Edmond stepped in before the King could respond.

"If I may Your Majesty, I would advise you do nothing about the man for now. We don't know if he is the new leader or not yet. Lord Dafydd has just recently died in battle, and I am sure there will be an election of sorts to find a new leader before long. But until we hear anything about a new leader I think we should leave those people alone for the time being," he said.

"I don't know if there will be any kind of election," Sir Stanley said. "Llywelyn is a true born leader if you ask me."

"Even if that is true we won't know anything for a while yet. So let's leave them alone for now, Lord Edmond implored.

"You must all be starving after your journey. Let us retire to the dining hall for supper and we can continue this discussion later," the King said standing up. The Prince and the two older men followed, and they left the room together.

Chapter 21

One True Leader

Aberfraw Castle, Gwynedd, Wales

Dafydd the younger rode up to the castle gates on his way back from town. He quite often liked to go into town and check out the marketplace and see the different things on sale there. It had been a favorite pastime of his since he was a young boy. The air in the town always smelled of chimney smoke, and when he passed the taverns he could always catch the whiff of hops from the ale being brewed there. Being among the people of the town, he felt more like a normal person and less like royalty.

He reached the castle gates and waved at the guard on the wall. The man waved back, and climbing down off the wall came to open the gates.

"Back from the market are you?" the guard said with a knowing smile.

"Yes, as always," Dafydd said and rode through the gates into the courtyard beyond.

He rode to the door of the stable and dismounted. Then opening the door he led his pony inside. He led her into her stall and took off her saddle and bridle. Then he shut the stall door and hung up the saddle and bridle before throwing her some hay. He gave her a quick scratch on the side of the neck and then left the stables to find himself something to eat.

He walked into the courtyard to find his younger brother Rhodri there with a boy from the town.

"There you are," Rhodri said seeing him.

"What is going on?" Dafydd asked.

"The army has returned from war at last," Rhodri explained excitedly. "This young man came running up to the castle to tell someone when he saw me as I was coming to see if you had returned yet." The boy nodded his head in confirmation.

"Well, that would explain the air of excitement I felt in the town," Dafydd said.

"They are back?"

"Yes, and Elsa and her staff have already started preparing a homecoming feast for them. Let's go and meet them on the road and be the first to greet them," Rhodri said practically hopping up and down with excitement. Dafydd nodded in agreement and followed his brother and the boy back out of the front gates and back down the road towards town to greet the homecoming party, abandoning his plans to find something to eat. After all, there would be plenty to eat later. Elsa's feasts were always extravagant with lots of savory dishes, as well as ample amounts of brandy and beer. His mouth began to water just thinking about it.

Llywelyn rode into the town at the head of what was left of the Welsh army. Many of the soldiers along the way had left to return to their families and farms. Aside from himself and his brother Owain, there was Captain Carrol and several officers, as well as a small contingent of farmers from the village that bordered the outskirts of the town. These men made their farewells to Llywelyn and left to find their families and their beds.

In the town, children ran about the streets, and people came out of their houses and the taverns to watch Llywelyn and his companions passing. Some brave and bold children even ran up and tried to touch their swords that hung from their saddles. Llywelyn laughed at their antics and waved to their parents. Owain watched his brother and smiled to himself to see him so comfortable with the people. It was a good first step in becoming a leader.

"Can I buy you both a drink?" Carrol asked. Llywelyn shook his head.

"No, sorry. Maybe another time. I need to get back to the castle and see how things have been in my absence. It has only been my mother in charge, and I need to see how she is fairing with it all." Carrol nodded his head in understanding.

"Of course. Give her my best," he said.

"I will do that." Llywelyn agreed. "I am sure we will be seeing each other again soon." Carrol nodded and turned his horse's head in the direction of the nearest tavern. Several officers followed in his wake, while others left for their homes. This left Llywelyn alone with his brother and Olan. Without speaking they began moving through the streets once more in the direction of the road that led to the castle which could be seen from a distance.

The sight of the castle gave Owain a funny feeling. It had been so long since he had seen his home, and he felt both excited and nervous returning to it. The excitement he understood, but the nerves he didn't. He shrugged and tried not to think of anything at all as he followed his brother out of the town and onto the road.

Dafydd was the first to spot them as they came down the road and waved. Llywelyn saw them and pulled his horse to a halt. His brother and Olan followed suit behind him. The two boys ran up to them and stopped. Owain's heart filled with joy to see his brothers again, and he followed Llywelyn as he slid down from his horse onto the cobbles of the road to greet the boys. They pulled their brothers into a sort of group hug for a minute and then let go. Grinning at them with joy to see them again after so long.

"So, what happened?" Dafydd asked after they broke the hug.

"We will tell all later. Right now we just want to get back to the castle and rest. Why don't you two hop on behind us and we can get back faster," Llywelyn suggested. The boys nodded in agreement and climbed up behind their two older brothers. Then they started back to the castle once more.

"Did we win?" Rhodri asked unable to help himself.

"Yes, we won," Owain confirmed.

"Are you serious?" Dafydd asked surprised.

"Yes," Llywelyn said with a smile at the surprise in his brother's voice.

"Well then there is even more reason to celebrate," Dafydd said with a smile of his own.

"Celebrate?" Llywelyn asked confused.

"Elsa has been putting her staff to work preparing a homecoming feast for you," Dafydd explained.

"Oh, she didn't have to do that."

"She is happy to know you have returned safely, and so am I. I am so excited that you are home that I don't know what to say."

Llywelyn smiled.

"You don't need to say anything. Just knowing you are happy to see us is good enough," he said.

"I wonder what mother will say when she hears the news of our victory," Owain said. Dafydd and Rhodri exchanged an uncomfortable look before Rhodri turned away and focused his gaze on the back of Owain's head instead.

"What is it?" Llywelyn asked feeling the sudden change in their energy.

"Do you want me to tell them?" Dafydd asked looking at his little brother. Rhodri nodded while keeping his eyes averted.

"What?" Dafydd cleared his throat. He felt a little strange speaking into the back of his brother's head, so he tried to turn his face to see them all more clearly.

"Mother passed away," he said simply.

"What? When?" Owain asked.

"About two weeks ago. We buried her next to grandfather," Dafydd explained.

"It would appear that we have a lot to talk about," Llywelyn said as they reached the castle gates.

"Later." His three brothers nodded in agreement.

The gates were opened by the guard on the wall and they rode through into the courtyard beyond. They stopped in the middle of the courtyard and slid down from the saddle. Olan took the reins of Owain and Llywelyn's horses and rode off in the direction of the stables, leaving the four brothers alone. Together they walked up to the front doors of the castle and through into the castle beyond.

They started walking through the castle halls in the direction of their rooms to change and get ready for the homecoming feast.

"So what exactly happened with mother?" Llywelyn asked.

"She had a terrible cough," Dafydd explained.

"It sounded like her bones were rattling in her chest when she breathed," Rhodri added with a shudder at the memory of the sound.

"It is too bad we couldn't have buried father there as well," Owain said.

"Do you know where they buried him after his body was taken away?" Llywelyn asked. Owain shook his head.

"I assumed he was buried close to the prison where they bury all their dead. But I am not a hundred percent on that," he said.

"I am happy you two were here for her at least," Llywelyn said giving his two younger brothers a weak smile. He felt like the floor had become a great lake and he was sinking into it and was unsure he would be able to keep his head above water for very long. He didn't know how much more he could take. He felt like his whole world had been turned upside down and that he had no control and was just along for the ride. Slowly everyone he had looked up to had been taken away from him. First his grandfather, and then his father followed by his uncle, and now his mother. Who would be next? Would he lose his brothers as well? He shook himself mentally. He was being crazy. His brothers were young and strong and would be around for a long time he told himself. But he couldn't hide his fear of what the future might bring.

Later that evening at the feast, Llywelyn ate and drank with the rest of the castle's inhabitants along with many other nobles that lived in the area who had come to congratulate him for such a victory. But he still felt numb. The food had little taste and he felt he was simply eating and drinking out of formality. It was too bad because Elsa had outdone herself, but he was just too exhausted to notice much.

He didn't notice his brother sit down next to him until he placed his hand on his shoulder.

"You look exhausted. You need sleep," Owain said squeezing his shoulder.

"You are right. Can you give them all my apologies?" Owain nodded, and standing up, Llywelyn left the great hall to get some much needed sleep. The way he was feeling he thought he could sleep for a hundred years. But he would settle for at least one night in a comfortable bed.

The next morning the four brothers left the castle to travel to the royal burial ground. Several generations of the ruling families of Gwynedd were buried there. The place was incredibly quiet and peaceful as they walked through the graves reading the names on the headstones. Some were so old that the names were illegible, but others were still clear enough to read.

After a time they found the two fresh graves of their grandfather and their mother and kneeling they each placed a white stone upon each of the graves to show they had been there. Neither of them spoke afraid to break the peace of the place. But after a time, they all stood as one and left the graveyard together.

"Are you okay?" Owain asked looking at his brother.

Llywelyn nodded. "Yes, I am all right. It is just a shock to see that grave. It makes it more real somehow."

Owain nodded his head in agreement. "I know what you mean," he said as they began to walk back towards the castle. "Have you thought any more about what you are going to do?"

"What do you mean?"

"I mean have you thought any more about becoming the leader of Gwynedd?"

Llywelyn shrugged. "I still don't know. I am afraid I don't have what it takes to do it." Owain stopped walking and Llywelyn stopped as well.

"Look at my face," Owain said. "Is this the face of a man who would lie to you?"

"You are many things my brother, but a liar is not one of them," Llywelyn said.

"So then listen to me and believe me when I say that you, Llywelyn ap Gruffudd are the best man to lead this great land of ours. You are smart and strong, and men have always followed you. No one else could have rallied the troops the way you did, and it is because of you that we won the war against a much larger army. Face it, you are our one true leader."

"But how am I supposed to lead us? Sure I have military experience, but that means nothing. I am young and untested, and I don't see how that could be a good quality in a leader."

"You will learn as you go," Owain said. "Yes, you are young, but that also means you are not set in your ways yet. You will find your own ways to make things work for you as a leader. Everyone is different, but that isn't a bad thing."

"You will be by my side?"

"Every step of the way," Owain said with a smile. Llywelyn nodded and began walking back down the road to the castle once more. Owain fell into step beside him and they walked along in silence, each alone with their thoughts.

Maybe his brother was right. Maybe he was the right man for the job. Maybe it was like he said that he just had to find out what would work for him. He was crazy. Taking on such a venture would mean his life would never be the same again. But was that necessarily a bad thing? Maybe not. After all, his life had already changed so much that what was wrong with a little more? He smiled to himself as he realized that he had made his choice. He would do it. He would become the ruler of Gwynedd and lead his people the best he could to honor the memories of his parents and his grandfather. With a slightly lighter heart, he walked back through the gates. He walked through the front doors into the castle and went to go and find something to eat for breakfast with his three brothers beside him, reminding him that not all of his family was gone.

About the Author

Sydney has a big imagination and has been writing and performing from a young age. After going blind from Leukemia at the age of three, she found release from the medical part of her life through her music and her writing. In high school she excelled in English and history and after she left school she continued to write and to create her music. She formed her band, The Undercurrents with her best friend and drummer, Alex Nacci at the age of 22 and has been playing music with the band ever since. Her book, Princes and Kings, is her first professional novel and it is book one of the historical fiction series she is writing titled, A Rose in A Thorn Bush about the last king of Wales. She was introduced to her main character in high school and with the encouragement of her Business Abilities coach she finely decided to write his story. Splitting the story into three books. Sydney has always enjoyed reading historical fiction and has found it an interesting genre to write in. After her series is finished she plans to continue writing about different historical British characters for as long as she can. Being Welsh on her father's side and Scottish and English on her mother's Britain is a place that interests her greatly and she has enjoyed writing about one of its characters. Giving her a chance to explore her heritage in a fun and exciting way and she looks forward to sharing her passion for the genre and the history of the British Isles with the world.

Manufactured by Amazon.ca
Bolton, ON

20715533R00155